THE ROYAL TARGET

HOUSE OF SOZZINI - BOOK 1

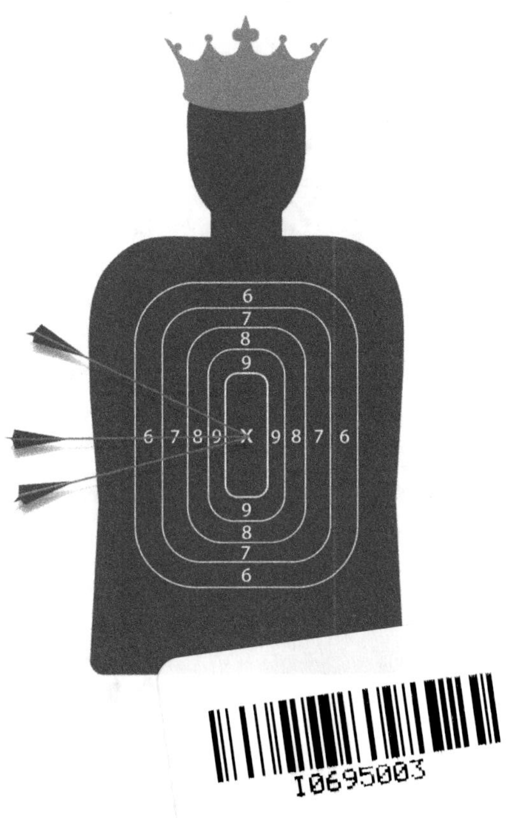

L. BETH CAMPBELL

The Royal Target

HOUSE OF SOZZINI

BOOK ONE

L. BETH CAMPBELL

Copyright © 2025 by L. Beth Campbell

All rights reserved.

No part of this book may be reproduced in any form or by any electronic or mechanical means, including information storage and retrieval systems, without written permission from the author, except for the use of brief quotations in a book review.

ISBN-13: 978-1-960639-17-2

Cover Art and Cover Layout by L. Beth Campbell

This is a work of fiction. Any similarities to real people, living or dead, are merely coincidental.

lbethcampbell.com

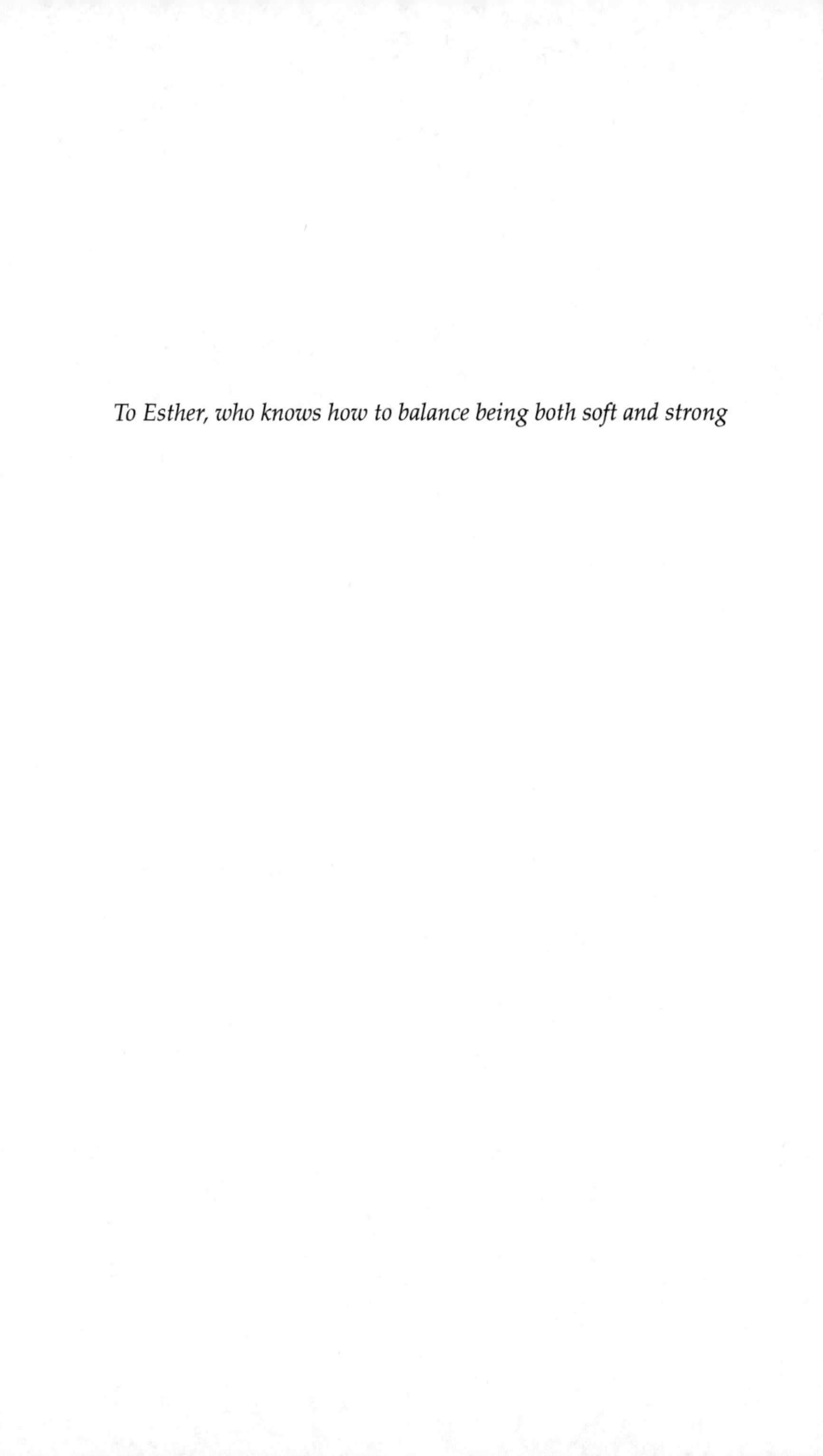

To Esther, who knows how to balance being both soft and strong

"Again." I've heard that word so many times throughout my training that the mantra of it has become ingrained in my subconscious, even when I sleep at night.

"Again." Good, but not great.

"Again." Great, but not perfect.

"Again." For the mission, it has to be perfect.

"Again." There are no second chances on a quest this dangerous.

"Again." Only the best get to go, and I've proven through the grit of sore muscles and achy bones that no one else but me has the tenacity to succeed and survive.

Dario hands me my water bottle after the round of drills through the military-style obstacle course. Given the twists and turns that exist on the streets of our city, it's not hard to imagine the types of escapes I might have to pull off for the mission. Climbing over walls isn't out of the question for me. Some agents are sent as spies to collect information, but my training is specialized.

The Resistance officially formed when those who were questioning the validity of the monarchy united and chose a leader. Their distrust stirred them to calculated action when King Vincenzo attacked a powerful duke's estate. Initially, the organization was backed by an unnamed noble family, but several others have joined since. They strategically established their headquarters in the island city of Venezia on the opposite coast of the royal castle. Though I'm curious about the locations and titles of our allies, knowing wouldn't be relevant to my current life. Given the risk that I could be captured on my mission, I shouldn't know those details. The King of Lazio doesn't seem to take kindly to possible betrayers. All I can guess is that my biological parents were caught in the crossfire.

I was eight when the Resistance decided to recruit me for their school and training program. Every year, my class would undergo a strict evaluation, one that always cuts the remaining group in half. By the time I was sixteen, I was the only remaining candidate. In hindsight, that was the easy part. When all the training—all the pressure—was focused on one point, it forced me to either break or do what it took to get stronger. I quickly learned that the best way to survive is to make sure that breaking is never an option. Though he's the last person to show me sympathy six days of the week, it's on the seventh day, my designated rest and recovery day, that Dario transforms from my relentless coach into one of my two best friends.

The Resistance assigned Dario as my guide, and at the same time, I was given high-level information about my ultimate mission. He was my mentor when I started the training program, but the mission demanded a new level of commitment. By choosing my close friend, they were betting that he would know exactly how to push me to my greatest potential in a way that a stranger would take months to figure out. Dario is often kind, but he's also stubborn and resilient.

Six days of strength training, cardio endurance, archery, shooting range, hand-to-hand combat, and memorizing every nook and cranny of the capital city are routinely followed by a day off. Holidays are no exception. Although I thrive under the pressure, I live for those days off.

CHAPTER 1

Adelina

I often spend my days off near one of the many canal bridges scattered throughout the island city as Dario rows his family's gondola. His short curls are temporarily bleached blond from the hours of constant sunlight during our summer training sessions. His sun-kissed, golden skin, honey-brown eyes, and sculpted muscles are a fan favorite among females in our age group. A few years ago, their unabashed stares were coupled with glares of jealousy in my direction. I'm the girl whose job it is to spend hours every day with the man whom they consider to be the most eligible bachelor. To me, though, he's the closest thing I have to a brother.

The girls who used to stand here in attempts to catch his attention all set their sights on other gondoliers when the news spread that Dario had fallen completely in love with another girl, my sister and my other best friend. Our schedule isn't exactly conducive to normal dating and relationships; Maria slipped through the cracks of the walls he put up for years.

Though they're not my biological parents, Maria's parents raised me as their own, which makes us practically sisters.

With less than a year separating our ages, we were in the same classes at school before I was enrolled at the training academy. Maria was the one who always had ice packs ready for me when I got home late after a long practice session. She would set backup alarms for me whenever I had important exams and evaluations. Without her in my support system, I wouldn't have made it through the academy's high standards. We're so connected that I don't have to look to know it's her when I sense someone sitting down next to me.

"He looks so peaceful when he's on the water," she says with a lovesick sigh. My two friends being in love is both wonderful and somewhat nauseating at the same time.

"He could be punching someone in the face and still look peaceful," I say, diverting my eyes back to the map of the castle hidden in my book. Any innocent onlooker would think I'm an avid reader, but on a regular rotation, I frequently switch the various escape routes with different books from Maria's small literary collection.

After a few moments of silence, she says, "I wish you would actually read some of these books rather than using them as a cover for your extracurricular studies. I mean, you've spent countless hours holding and carrying around literary classics without reading any of the words. I know you don't believe me when I tell you this, but there are things you can learn from reading those novels." When my dark brown eyes meet her hazel ones, I can see the concern she thinks she hides well. I was eight the first time I saw that glint in her eye, the one that expresses she will always worry about me.

My mind centers back on the present moment as Dario makes the leap from the gondola onto the small pier nearby. A smile is plastered across his face as Maria blushes. It's a scene that seems straight out of one of the romance novels that Maria enjoys reading during holiday breaks. I only had to read one to assume that they all must be similar in plot. I divert my eyes back to the map I came here to refresh my memory on. Instead, my motivation seems to have vanished with the arrival of my friends.

"Dario, please tell her that it's okay to take a break from her preparation on her one day off during the week," Maria says to him as she breaks away from his hug. She rarely tries to use him against me, so I close the book and put it back in my crossbody satchel.

Dario merely shrugs, unable to take sides in this argument. When her attention is elsewhere, he gives me a reassuring wink. After all, he's the one who taught me the book trick to hide my study obsession from curious stares. Most people my age don't study maps in their free time, and I got tired of strangers asking what I was doing.

We walk toward the plethora of restaurants that decorate the riverside of the Canal Grando. Through an unspoken agreement, the three of us regularly rotate who chooses where we eat lunch, and today is Dario's turn. Unlike Maria and me, who have our favorites that we tend to frequent, Dario makes a habit of making us try somewhere different every third week. His attempts only go so far, though, because I've mastered the art of ordering the same thing from any place he brings us to. Maria used to do the same, but Dario has slowly helped encourage her out of her comfort zone. Rather than try the same tactic on me, he lets me take comfort in my routine because any day now, my mission will start, and my life will drastically change. Forever. Or maybe, finishing this mission will be when my life can finally begin.

Many of our history books talk about a time when our city was overrun with tourists from all over the world for at least half the year. The text is supplemented by photos showing crowds so thick you would have to push your way through to get anywhere quickly. Just the idea of that is baffling to me when I think about how our small streets and canals create a maze that even local children get lost in.

The first map I memorized was of all the streets and canal bridges, especially the general area between the Canal Grando and the Piasa San Marco. Now at the age of twenty-three, I could find my way through the city blindfolded. Literally, for a section of my training, Dario blindfolded me and tested my ability to figure out my location and navigate to the destination without using my eyes. He repeatedly told me, "If you can find your way in this city, you'll never get lost in the capital." At least I've never had to find my way while also avoiding running over bumbling tourists who don't speak our language. Looking around at the city's beauty, I can see why it was chosen to disguise the headquarters of the Resistance.

HALF AN HOUR after I've finished the rock climbing speed drill, I wrap my sore fingers in preparation for the hour of kickboxing that awaits me. Dario and I are ten minutes into our drills when I notice the director of the Resistance standing by the door. Within seconds, Dario sees her too and stops to give her his full attention.

"Director Verde," Dario says to her with a nod of acknowledgement. She's wearing the same outfit combination that she wore the last dozen times I saw her, consisting of a crisp white button-up blouse and perfectly tailored black trousers. Her shoes are the only part of her appearance that differs—blue patent leather ballet flats today, rather than the red suede loafers she has worn multiple times. The change in footwear isn't the only difference today, though. Across her face is a bright smile, a stark contrast to her usual straight face of seriousness. It's a sign of good news.

"Dario, Adelina, I like what I'm seeing here," she addresses us. I internally cringe as I try to calculate how long she must have been standing there watching before either of us picked up on her presence. Given how much it's been drilled into me to be always aware of my surroundings, I should have been able to feel her the moment she walked in the room. My internal self-chiding stops when I remember that Dario didn't sense her until after I had, and Dario is one of the best. Except, I'm not supposed to be just one of the best; I'm supposed to be *the* best. The never-ending question is whether I'll ever feel as if I'm living up to the expectation.

Never one to dwell on compliments from authority figures nor beat around the bush, Dario asks, "Any updates on the timing of the mission?"

"We've just received word that the royal family is hosting a ball in honor of the prince's twenty-fifth birthday," Director Verde reports with her eyes locked on me. "Two weeks from this Friday. Will you be ready by then?"

The *you* in her inquiry is singular, clearly directed at me, though Dario is the one who replies, "She's ready."

"Franco is going to be your backup and partner on this mission. He's currently making the traveling preparations," she informs us, confirming what I had long suspected. Originally, before Dario and Maria's romance began, Dario was meant to be my partner to the capital and into the castle. He's never confirmed that he requested a replacement, but Maria has hinted here and there that he wouldn't be leaving the city of Venezia on any planned assignments. While having him by my side for the majority would ease the nerves, I could never live with myself if he became a casualty. Franco is the next best option. He's as skilled and disciplined as Dario when he chooses to be.

Director Verde doesn't have many details yet, besides the departure two Thursdays from now, but she leaves with the promise of bringing more information tomorrow. Once Dario is certain she's far enough away not to overhear, he says to me with his voice thick with guilt, "I wanted to tell you sooner that I won't be accompanying you."

"I assumed that you weren't," I tell him. "Once I could see that things were serious with my sister, I knew you couldn't be the one to come with me. If things don't go as planned, she can't lose both of us." Though I'd had that thought countless times, saying the words out loud feels like a confession and admission that I might not come out of this alive.

"Lina, you're going to succeed, and you're going to come back to us," Dario insists, his hands on my shoulders as he forces me to face him.

How Dario can be so certain of my ability baffles me. This is everything I've been working toward since I was only eight, but the mission had always seemed like a lofty goal that would never arrive. The concrete reality comes crashing toward me like the waves after a storm, the tide that floods our streets during the rainy seasons. I'm leaving in two and a half weeks, and I have no idea what life looks like when I return. But I can't comprehend the *after* until it's over—until I've succeeded and survived. I take a deep breath before responding. "We both know that this could very well fail."

"You're a survivor. You survived as a baby when your parents sacrificed their lives to get you somewhere safe."

No one ever talks about my biological parents, mostly because no one knows who they were or anything about them. When I was five, Maria's parents explained to me that someone brought me to them as a baby and that my parents loved me enough to help me escape whatever danger they were in. No one ever showed up here claiming to be my parents, so after a few years, we assumed they were killed. For all I know, they may still be out there somewhere.

"Considering how much we don't know about them, I don't think that's a logical argument," I retort as I grab my bag from the hook on the wall where I'd hung it this morning.

"You have to return," he insists again. "Maria is going to need a maid of honor at our wedding." I freeze as his words register in my mind. I knew he had been acting suspiciously the past few weeks.

"When are you proposing?" I ask him, suddenly giddy with excitement.

"Tonight."

HE'S SNEAKY; I'll give him that. Leave it to Dario to choose a proposal idea that makes it exceedingly difficult for me to spy on them—his family's gondola. The diverging canals are hard to follow and track from the streets and bridges, but I treat this opportunity as if it's the penultimate challenge. It's one thing to remain within earshot consistently enough to catch the moment, but it's another entirely to do so without Dario seeing me. Dressed in all black, I hide out near the small pier where his family docks their gondola and wait for Maria's voice.

Vibrant shades of tangerine and magenta paint the sky as lights across the city begin to flicker on, their reflections mingling in a dance with the sunset's counterpart in the canal waters. Venezia is at its most beautiful and captivating between sunset and dusk, the time when the sky isn't completely dark, but the lights awaken for their shift. If the city during the day is full of adventure, night is when it bursts with romance. I hear Maria's soft giggle as Dario guides her to the gondola that he's taken her on several times before.

I'd shown up here intending to follow them, but as Dario propels the boat away from the pier and down the narrow canal, I abort my plan in exchange for my favorite habit. I wind my way through the streets and over bridges until the small walkway opens up to reveal the Piasa San Marco. The restaurants that line the outside of the piazza all have tables set out, and live classical music drifts over the air, much like the birds in spring. My heart aches as I remember that my time here for the foreseeable future is coming to an end soon. Despite Dario's well-meaning pep-talk, he and I both know that in the best-case scenario, I still can't return to Venezia right away. At the risk of being followed, the route back home is drawn out so that Franco and I don't accidentally lead one of the king's men to the main headquarters of the Resistance. The prolonged return also acts to display our victory to our allies across various cities.

I slow down and deepen my breath as if taking in more of the cool, crisp air will allow my body to absorb more of this feeling to take with me. The atmosphere here is almost magical every time I come at this time of day. On my days off, I frequent here at the second-best time to see the square— sunrise—and enjoy an overpriced cup of espresso. My eyes begin to water when the violinist strums the opening notes of my favorite song, a lullaby that always soothed me as a child. I've always imagined it was the song my birth mother would hum to me at night, back before I had this life.

"I told you she would be here," I hear Maria's voice say behind me. I turn around to see the newly engaged couple beaming and practically floating in a rush to tell me the official news.

"Let me see the ring," I say to her without trying to act surprised. Maria pauses to pout at Dario for telling me in advance before stretching out her left hand to me. The small diamond on the family heirloom catches and refracts the light from a nearby lantern. The jewelry that's been passed down for generations in his family looks like it was made for her, the way that she's made for him. A perfect fit if there ever was one.

"I thought you would try to follow us and eavesdrop on the whole proposal," Dario admits sheepishly. "I half expected you to meet us at the pier."

Maria throws him a look that means, "I told you so," which is an expression he'd better become accustomed to. I decide to bail him out this time. "That's exactly what I was going to do. But I didn't want to pass up the opportunity to enjoy the sunset here."

Maria catches something in my statement or my tone, and her confusion hits me like a knife. I didn't want her to reschedule her date with Dario tonight, so I opted to tell her after the proposal. For the same reasons, he must not have mentioned anything to her yet either. Dario and I make eye contact as if that will help us decide how to break the news to her. Before we can communicate it nonverbally, she asks me, "How soon are you leaving?"

"Two weeks from Thursday," the four words escape from my mouth. I look at my sister with pleading eyes, begging her to let this go until we can talk privately later. If she delves into this now, I might cry, and I don't cry in public. "Right now is about the two of you and your upcoming marriage and how even in a crazy world, love exists."

"Lina, do you want to grab dinner with us?" Dario asks me, but I know it's out of politeness more than anything. I shouldn't be a third wheel on their celebratory date.

"No, go ahead without me," I insist to both of them. "I'm going to head home and have dinner there. I want to take advantage of home-cooked meals while I can. Maria, I'll wait up and we can talk when you get home."

"You don't have to go if you don't want to," Maria says once she's closed our bedroom door. "I'm sure one of the other agents is capable of doing the same job."

"Maria, you and I both know that this has to be me," I say to her as gently as I can muster. "None of the other female operatives are skilled enough, and this has to be done by a woman. All the intel we have points to the fact that he's likely in search of a wife soon, so someone like me is bound to be less suspecting."

She gives a small chuckle with a shake of her head before she responds, "That prince will take one look at you and be defenseless. Especially if he's as secluded from the outside world as everyone claims."

"I doubt that, considering a prince has his choice of anyone in the Kingdom," I say with an eye roll. "If the guys in this city don't notice me, a prince isn't likely to either."

"Lina, the reason why none of the guys in Venezia have paid you any attention is because they know you're off-limits until after the mission, even if they don't know what the mission is," Maria explains. "There have been a few who aren't intimidated by you that Dario had to ward off because none of us can afford for you to become distracted. But when you come back, you'll be able to find what I found in him. I want that for you, you know. A partner, a family of your own. A life outside of the martial arts, rock climbing, archery, and whatever else you and Dario spend your time doing six days a week. You'll be coming home to a new beginning."

Maria's speech voiced the very fears I've managed to delay about what comes after. As uncertain as my assignment has been, the future is less clear. The idea of my own marriage and children seems foreign compared to the feel of the bow and arrow in my hands. It's hard to make plans or dream about what lies ahead when the thing that lies between me and that part of my life is the assassination of the prince.

CHAPTER 2

Niccolò

I hate birthdays. I haven't always despised the celebration of my birth, but since I was fifteen, it's been the marker of time that my father uses to proclaim all the ways in which I'm failing. I was eleven when my mother passed away after weeks of illness—the moment that the innocence of childhood died with her last breath. Between eleven and fifteen, though life wasn't the same without her warmth and kindness, it was still bearable. But the unthinkable happened when my older brother died in a freak accident. Rumors still float around about whether my brother planned it as a means to escape my father. While I can't blame him for wanting to leave all this behind, he never would have left me alone with that man—the king.

My father has never been forthcoming with his love for anyone but my mother, himself, and his power. I was never supposed to be the crown prince of the kingdom, but Carlo's untimely demise left my ruthless father with only one remaining heir. His cruelty may be his strategy to toughen me, or it's his way of grieving my mother as if my remaining existence were punishment for his crimes. When he looks at me, he sees her deep blue eyes rather than his hard gray ones that Carlo had inherited. I'm too much like her, and that's become my burden to bear.

This huge birthday celebration is just another way in which my father is trying to keep up appearances. The last thing he wants to do is reveal any weaknesses or flaws. Showing me off to the world in such a public way is his version of declaring that, despite the tragedies of years past, the royal line is stronger than ever. It's a grand illusion to hide his increasing fears about the growing restlessness among the people and the rumors about the Resistance. Though he claims they are only rumors when asked, I know the truth. I suspect the Resistance will have some of their agents in attendance at the ball to either scope out the security at the castle for a future attack or to make an assassination attempt that very night. If I were them, I would choose the latter.

At first, when he suggested a large party to commemorate my twenty-fifth birthday, I thought it was his way of encouraging me to meet eligible ladies around my age. Marry, have an heir of my own, secure the royal line once again. Logically, that strategy makes the most sense. Realistically, he should have pushed me in that direction years before now, but he never once brought up the idea of marriage in any of his conversations. Surely the importance of my producing an heir has crossed his mind.

"Your father always has a reason for what he both does and doesn't do," my mother used to remind me. A month ago, I searched through the laws and records for why he would withhold that particular instruction and encouragement from me. Finally, I located a contract that had been enacted when I was two, back when I was merely the "spare prince." My father's signature and seal confirmed the document's significance. I quickly scanned the pages for names and references that seemed familiar to me when my body went rigid. I read and re-read the legal jargon on repeat until I was sure that my brain or eyes hadn't made a mistake. Words such as "Prince Niccolò Mattei of the House of Mattei of the Kingdom of Lazio" and "official betrothal." The less familiar phrases were almost more concerning to me, though.

When my father had deemed it appropriate for me to begin my royal studies to take my brother's place (precisely seventy-two hours after we buried his body), my tutor insisted that I know the kingdom's laws like the back of my hand. To this day, my memory can recall the most obscure and seemingly useless laws. For the previous few generations, betrothals have been few and far between. Rather than force their children to marry someone for political gain, the royal families use the subtle tactic of restricting their offspring's social life to those of similar upbringing and status. In the Kingdom of Lazio, a betrothal is as legally binding as marriage and can only be annulled with proof of the death of one or both parties.

The eldest daughter of Alessandro and Valentina Sozzini of the House of Sozzini of the Kingdom of Lazio. My legally betrothed, a woman I had never met to my knowledge, is the other party on the contract. Though the name sounds familiar, I know they're not on the list of current noble families. I wrote down those words on a piece of paper, sensing that the only way forward from here is to find out what happened to the noble family of the House of Sozzini.

When I was given a copy of the invitation list for the ball, I scrutinized every name, hoping that maybe they were a low-key family not worth mentioning by my tutors. I exhausted every option I could think of on my own, but the sole lead I could find was an announcement released a few months after the betrothal contract about the birth of a daughter to Alessandro and Valentina. All traces of their family seem to have vanished, almost as if they never existed beyond the moment of lifelong promise and confirmation of a daughter. I pulled some strings to search the death certificates in the Kingdom for the name Sozzini, but all were issued before her birth. Her birth certificate was also missing from the records, as if someone wanted to make sure she could never be found. I just so happened upon one of the greatest mysteries, and it is tied to my life in a way my father didn't bother to tell me.

At breakfast today, I consider asking him and revealing all I've discovered, but something in my gut tells me that there's a reason why what little information there is has been cleverly disguised. I wouldn't put it past that man to have been responsible for the disappearance of my betrothed and her family. Perhaps they were secretly part of the Resistance, or maybe they knew something that could cause others to question his right and ability to rule. The fact that there was even a contract between my family and hers might have been his way of trying to bribe them. After all, any noble family would be thrilled to have their daughter become a princess, even if it's not to the crown prince. If they had that much influence, my father is the only one who could have been a threat to them. All the theories and conspiracies haunt me as speculations go unanswered within the walls of this castle.

In two weeks, these stone walls that have been my prison will be filled with onlookers here to satiate their curiosity under the guise of celebrating me. Since the death of my brother, my father has kept me out of the public eye, perhaps to protect me—to protect his bloodline. Last year, I overheard a royal advisor inform my father that the public speculates my lack of publicity is due to an illness. Personally, I don't care what the gossips have to say regarding my health. The truth would have come out eventually because my father can't live forever.

While the castle workers hustle to prepare, I make preparations of my own. This event isn't just an opportunity for the king to show off his strong heir, but it's an opportunity for me to make my escape from the castle when hundreds of others are leaving after the party. Each day, I mentally scour every strategy and possible route to not only escape but also remain undetected by my father for a few weeks. If I'm right about my father's actions driving them away, my only hope to find someone from the House of Sozzini requires a carefully thought-out course.

I INSPECT my tailored navy suit and take a few deep breaths. While the castle staff has been checking and double-checking that everything is in place, I've been ensuring that I've upheld my end of the preparations for the night. Though I'm in a separate wing of the castle, the low rumble of guests in the main ballroom can be heard from my usually quiet chamber. A knock sounds at the door before my father's right-hand man, Georgio, appears.

"Your Highness, five minutes until your introduction to your guests," he informs me as he waits to escort me. I meet his stride as he guides me to the entrance specifically designated for the introduction of nobility. Butterflies swarm my insides as the seconds seem to inch by. Through the ornate wooden doors, I can hear the vivacious sounds of laughter and conversation accompanied by the live orchestra. The dancing isn't scheduled to begin for another half hour, but I can already picture the dance floor filled with couples twirling and waltzing. It's been so long since I've practiced a waltz that I had to ask someone to help me freshen up on it this past week. All at once, I hear the roar go silent as the doors swing open. "His Royal Highness, the Prince of Lazio," the announcer says as all eyes focus on me.

The first few seconds are eerily silent as the crowd takes in the appearance of their future king. Slowly, the guests resume whatever action they were in the middle of before, and I notice a few clusters of women, both young and old, whispering as they pretend not to stare. While I'm precisely what some expected, I'm sure those who were riding the theory of an ill prince are disappointed to see I'm as strong and healthy as any other man my age, maybe even stronger.

I gracefully descend the steps onto the main floor, only to pause at the bottom. I'm at the largest and most elaborate party of the decade, and I don't recognize anyone here apart from my father and his attendants at the table reserved for the royal family—if he and I alone can be considered much of a family anymore. It's bizarre being a stranger at my own birthday party.

I scan various groups near me for any hint of recognition. I wasn't a social recluse until my brother died, so some of my friends from my childhood should be around here somewhere. Ten years can change a person, both physically and in personality.

"Well, it looks like you grew into that big head of yours after all," a deep voice says on my left. It's both recognizable and unknown to me, but the features of his face instantly jog my memory when I turn to look at my former best friend.

"It's been much too long, Antonio," I say as relief floods my body to see his smile. I'm surprised to find that he's an inch shorter than me after all those years that he was the tall one among our group of friends. Despite that, though, he's transformed into a man the same way I have over the past decade.

He teases, "Hey, that's Duke of Genoa now. But I'll let you be an exception since I'd rather not call you 'Your Highness' every time I address you." He extends his hand to me as a gesture of friendliness. The other three men he was talking to introduce themselves, all names that I recall, even if their faces weren't as easy for me to remember as my closest friend's had been. Another lifetime ago, we had adventures together the way young boys do. The last time any of them had seen me, I wasn't the crown prince, and the difference in how they address me shows, except for Antonio.

Gradually, they relax as they discuss the things they must talk about at all the various social events they're obligated to attend: women. It becomes clear to me that none of them have married yet as they discuss their recent affairs and whether any of the currently single noble ladies are worth giving up their freedoms for. I stand there and listen while observing the other types of guests.

At the corner of one of the large windows overlooking the courtyard are older ladies, likely with unmarried daughters who are also in attendance. They're unapologetic in how they're scrutinizing me, possibly plotting how they can force me to dance with their daughters.

Meanwhile, my father has a long line of noblemen pretending to mingle while waiting to speak with him, although they are all clearly in line. As he's told me, "The married men only have two reasons to come to a ball. The first is that their wives and daughters wanted to come. The second is that it allows them to gain face time with me without trying to make an appointment. I'll usually entertain whatever need they have for a few minutes before dismissing them for whoever is next in the queue." He wasn't making that up.

I decide to excuse myself to get a glass of wine and explore the food options when my body shifts and collides with another. My reflexes are quick enough to keep me upright on my feet, but not fast enough to catch the woman who falls on the floor beside me. I kneel to check on her and offer my help.

"I'm so sorry," I apologize, and my entire soul seems to reel at the sight of her. Her gown is a fiery red contrast against her olive skin and dark hair that cascades in voluminous curls. She's breathtaking, and for a split second, I feel as if I were the one who had fallen on the floor. I regain my composure as I help her up.

Her dark chocolate brown eyes meet mine as she says, "No, I'm sorry. I should have been watching where I was going." Even the timbre of her voice is lovely. I want to hear her speak again.

"The dancing hasn't started yet, but would you give me the honor of a dance?" I ask her, and the conflict is evident on her face. I quickly add, "It is my birthday, after all," with the hopes that I've removed any excuse running through her head.

Resigned, she says, "Fine, one dance. Come find me when you're ready to claim it."

"Wait," I spurt out to stop her before she walks away. "I didn't catch your name, and it's only fair since mine was announced to the crowd."

She gives me a small smile and says, "Alessia. And technically, your name wasn't announced either; your title was."

As I watch her wander past other guests toward the dessert table, an impossible and illogical thought occurs to me. *Now I understand why a man would search his entire kingdom to find the owner of a glass slipper.* It's as if I'd never been fully alive until five minutes ago. It's wholly monumental with the worst possible timing. Everything inside me wants to chase her down and ensure she becomes a permanent fixture in my life, but I remember the contract my father had hidden away in the kingdom records. I can't properly pursue Alessia until I find out whether or not my betrothal is still valid. Not just that, but I don't know who Alessia is or what family line she comes from. In addition to the noble families, the palace hosted a lottery for commoners to win invitations to the ball. The guest list is so extensive that almost anyone could have snuck their way in here. I'm not just a man who's betrothed; I'm a prince with duties and responsibilities and a father who would get rid of anyone who stands in the way. I almost dread that I have to dance with her now that reality is sinking in.

I sip a glass of Moscato Giallo and eat a panino in hopes of settling my stomach. The first dance will be coming to an end soon, and before I can talk myself out of it, I spot Alessia and make my way toward her. People are so aware of my presence that they move out of my way, making it easy to reach her.

She watches me with an amused expression, taking some pleasure in how the man of the hour, the center of attention, can't seem to take his eyes off of her. Surely, she must be used to men behaving this way around her. I don't have to ask to know that the other unmarried guys in this room have taken notice of her. Just the idea of someone else winning her over causes jealousy to cloud my mind for a split second before I'm back in the present, my hand extended to her.

"Alessia, may I have this dance?" I ask her with stars in my eyes. Instead of the characteristic curtsy and nod that most ladies are taught, she smiles and gently places her hand in my outstretched one before linking her arm through mine. I guide her toward the collection of couples gathered in wait for the opening chords of the waltz. If she isn't of noble upbringing, she certainly dances as if she had been taught all her life. Something about her movements is more graceful than the others around us, smooth as if she has complete control over her body. Her eyes don't leave mine either as she follows my lead.

"Don't look now, but I think we've piqued your father's interest," she whispers nonchalantly. I peek a glance in his direction to find that she's right.

To anyone who hasn't spent twenty-five years deciphering that man's facial expressions, he appears indifferent, but I can see past the outward façade to his curiosity. It's not anger or excited curiosity, but near neutral. Rather than continue my inspection of his possible emotions, I take advantage of every second I get in Alessia's presence.

Faint freckles from spending time in the sun sprinkle her olive complexion. Her arms, only a quarter of which aren't hidden beneath the red fabric of her dress, are toned and muscular, not the delicate softness of the typical noblewoman. Then again, I haven't danced with any of the others to make a true comparison of how women are now.

Centuries ago, it was unheard of for most women to participate in any physical training, a trend that has changed as men began to see them as equals. I didn't know I had a preference for physically strong women until I saw Alessia. It means someone like her could keep up with me on an adventure.

"What do you think of this ball that my father decided to throw for me?" I ask her as a way to gauge whether she's enjoying herself or only tolerating me to appear well-mannered and gracious.

She gives my question a thought. A girl who thinks before she speaks is very appealing to me. "I think that he wants people to believe that he cares about you and cares about them. Part of him does care about you, but not enough to let you become your own person while he's still around. This ball is nice—don't get me wrong—but I suspect you had nothing to do with its planning." Bullseye. It's as if she read my mind when she gave me her thoughts, which is impressive given we're strangers.

"I did choose my suit," I point out to her. A navy velvet suit that I've never had any other occasion to wear until tonight. The song comes to an end. I bow as she curtsies to match the other couples participating in the waltz. Stealing what could be my last chance to make an impression, I escort her off the dance floor toward the table displaying plates of tiramisu.

I hand her a plate and a fork before grabbing one for myself, and she looks at it the way I've been looking at her all evening. She doesn't take a bite yet. "Don't ruin what was a good moment by trying to find me later," she says to me, almost pleading. "I'm not the kind of girl you want to have a future with. I'll stand here and eat cake with you. Then I'll wish you a happy birthday before I disappear. That way, you can spend time with other people here, like those friends you were talking to earlier. Take full advantage of this night."

I freeze at her words, the logical part of my head fully agreeing with her. It confirms my suspicion that she's not a noble. If I'd been smart, I would have started a conversation with an older duke or lord who is less fond of my father and intoxicated enough to reveal something about the House of Sozzini accidentally. Instead, I've been consumed by this beautiful distraction.

"I know you're likely right, but part of me doesn't want you to be," I sigh, preparing myself for the inevitable goodbye. She finishes her dessert in a few bites, hardly savoring the flavors the way I prefer to eat sweets. For whatever reason, she's in a rush now.

"It was nice meeting you," she says, and I can't decide whether she seems sad or pities me.

"The pleasure was all mine." I can tangibly feel when she's no longer in my vicinity, suddenly feeling alone in a room full of people. My good breeding takes over as I dance with a few ladies and engage with noblemen of various ages. There are subtle and obvious hints from mothers and fathers, as well as inquisitiveness regarding the mystery girl in red. By the time my father makes his exit from the party, I know I've fulfilled my social obligations for the night–hopefully for the year. It still takes a while to thank people for coming, and I give my old friends the promise that I'll stay in touch before I can slip out the doors into the main hall and head back to my chamber.

Weaving my way through the maze of hallways, I mentally run through the checklist of items I prepared. As I turn the corner that leads to my bedroom door, I pause when I see the door cracked open. Although I have a habit of closing my door, sometimes the staff forgets to close it completely. They've been so preoccupied with preparations for tonight that they're off their usual schedule. I turn on the light and find everything exactly where I had left it. Still, something feels off. The Resistance must have smuggled in their assassin after all. Though I can't be certain that someone is hiding, watching, and waiting for the opportunity to strike, I take the chance at the risk of sounding foolish.

"You know, killing me isn't going to stop my father from harming more innocent people," I reason out loud to seemingly nobody. When there's no response, I press on. "If I'm killed within the castle walls, he will stop at nothing until he's avenged the death of his only remaining heir. He's like a snake that only bites when he feels threatened. The kingdom will be a blood bath if he has a reason to attack. I have a better idea that delays a war the Resistance isn't prepared to win." I let my words hang in the air, patiently waiting for a sign that I'm not delusional.

After what feels like hours, a voice finally says, "Go on." But it's not just any voice. It's higher, more melodic, and so familiar that my head starts spinning. I shake my head to clear my thoughts. What point is charisma if you can't use it to convince your way out of your deathbed?

"You could take me with you," I say, hoping to hear her again to confirm my suspicions.

Alessia emerges out of the darkness of my connected bathroom, lowering her bow and arrow as she takes calculated steps toward me. She unsheathes the dagger at her thigh in a movement that's both practiced and elegant. Instead of the red gown she wore a couple of hours ago, she's now dressed in a black shirt and pants with her hair pulled back. The way her clothes fit accentuates all her curves, and the pieces and subtleties click into place. She's with the Resistance. All her weapons are designed to kill without noise.

"Why would I go through the trouble of kidnapping you when I can eliminate you right now?" she asks. "An assassinated heir would send a message to those who are undecided about which side they're on. It's one thing to take out the king in the open, but it's another to remove the heir he works so hard to protect."

"Because you won't be kidnapping me," I explain to her. As I'm saying it, it makes more sense. "I was planning on leaving tonight anyway, so I'll be going with you willingly. If you kill me here, soldiers will be after you within the hour, and the royal soldiers will be on high alert. But if I come with you, I'll leave a note telling my father that I wanted to get away to our vacation home in Napoli. It could take him a few weeks to realize I'm not where I said I am."

She starts pacing, her footsteps nearly silent on the marble floor. "Why would you want to leave?"

"Because I know the kind of man my father is, and I don't want to be anything like him," I tell her. While it is the truth, it's not the whole truth. Given the circumstances of the evening, I don't feel comfortable telling her about the disappearance of my betrothed. The Resistance exists because of the people who recognize that their king is corrupt. With a softer tone, I add the final reason, perhaps the most significant one of all. "I know you're not a killer. I've lived with one my whole life, and you're not like him."

She softens, and her shoulders relax. She sits down on the armchair near my fireplace, and I sit down in the matching one next to it. "If we're going to do this, I need to know exactly how you plan to leave undetected. So, what's your escape route?" she asks.

"I was going to leave a note for my father saying that I'm going to our vacation home and then take the hidden tunnel to the garage where my car is parked," I say simply with a shrug. "Nothing too elaborate."

"But wouldn't one of the staff at the vacation home inform someone that you're not there?"

"There is no full-time staff at the vacation home," I explain. "It's why I like to go there from time to time. We know people in that area who will clean it and stock it with food when I let them know ahead of time that I'll be staying there. It's the only place outside the castle that my father lets me go without question. So, I was going to drive my car down to the villa, park it there, and then leave after a day or two."

"That could work," she says thoughtfully. "But now, I have to be the one to drive your car because you haven't earned my trust yet."

CHAPTER 3

Adelina

Franco is going to freak out when he sees that the prince is not only alive and well, but he's also coming with us. Sort of. This is not what we were sent here to do. Within the shadows, I hurry to our rendezvous point to break the news to him. He's waiting underneath the stone pine, relief washing over his face when he sees that it's me.

"I was worried something had happened in there when you weren't back sooner," he says to me, starting in the direction of the car he drove us here in. Two seconds pass before he realizes I'm not walking with him. It must be written across my face because he asks, "You couldn't do it, could you?"

I feel a twinge of guilt as the full reality comes into view. Not only have I compromised my mission, but I've inadvertently dragged Franco into this confusing mess. I say the only thing to remedy the situation. "He's not like his father."

Those five words somehow convince him, though. He gives me a nod of approval and asks, "So then, straight back to Director Verde to give her the news? I'm sure she has a backup plan in mind for this scenario."

I'm hesitant to tell him the other part, the part about us going with the prince to his vacation home. Now that I'm away from him and in the fresh air, my mind is starting to doubt trusting the prince. This could be an elaborate scheme to trap us once we arrive at the supposed location. He could be working with his father to capture us, after all. Somehow, though, I trust the innocence I saw from the first moment our eyes locked. He had been kind and caring as he helped me up from the floor. And he certainly had been planning on leaving soon, given he already had a bag packed and ready. My training tells me that I should have stayed to read the note he's leaving, but it's too late. The only thing I have to go on right now is my gut.

"Actually, there's been a change of plans," I hedge before spilling the details I discussed with the prince from the second rendezvous point where he told me to meet him to the secluded house in Napoli that would serve as a resting point for us before ditching his car there and continuing on our original path back to Venezia.

I expect Franco to play devil's advocate and point out all the flaws and risks in this development, but instead, he says to me, "If you trust him, I trust him." Hearing my partner and backup in this say those words bolsters my confidence. He doesn't accuse me of wanting to trust the prince because he is handsome and charming. Franco trusts me to see beyond the outward glow of royalty and make a decision based on his character. The weight of the declaration isn't lost on me.

Franco drives our car while I give him directions to the meeting point that the prince had carefully described to me. It is a fifteen-minute drive from the castle, but still somehow on the castle grounds. Given how condensed things are in Venezia, it's baffling to me that one family can own this much land. A row of seven pairs of tall cypress trees lines either side of the path that leads to a large white gazebo. Franco waits in the car with the engine on and the windows down while I sit on the bench that follows the inner circle of the gazebo. There are faded drawings and carvings on the wood as if this were a popular play area for the young princes. The air here is slightly warmer than that of Venezia, and the night sky is brighter without all the lights to dim the radiance of the moon and stars.

Dim headlights appear before I can hear the crunch of tires on the dirt road. The prince stops his car next to where Franco is parked and rolls down his windows to peer at him.

"You'll be following behind me, right?" he asks Franco. Franco gives him a curt nod while remaining relaxed. "Let me give you the location in case anything happens and we get split up." Niccolò scribbles something on a piece of paper before he gets out of his car and walks to the driver's side, where Franco is waiting. At least this exchange isn't entirely unpleasant.

"I'm doing this because I trust her and her instincts," Franco tells him with warning in his voice.

Unshaken by the possible threat, the prince says to him, "Thank you," and then walks toward me.

"Did you get everything you need?" I ask him as I stride toward the driver's side of his car. I catch his nod as he strolls by my side. From a distance, I thought his sedan was black like the car Franco and I were given to use, but up close in the moonlight, the dark blue paint shimmers a shade reminiscent of the suit the prince had been wearing an hour ago. Before I can open the door, he's beside me with his hand on the handle, opening it for me. *Don't swoon,* I order myself. I sit myself on the luxury leather of the Maserati and adjust the seat and mirrors. I can survive three hours in the car with him, right?

I take a deep breath and note the locations of the various controls in this car. Already sitting and ready to go in the front passenger seat, he notices my hesitation. "You do know how to drive, don't you?" he says teasingly, shooting me a smile that probably got him out of trouble with his mom as a boy.

"Of course, I know how to drive." With all the hours I've spent training, driving is another skill I need to know in case of an emergency. Once every three months, we would travel off the island of Venezia to a driving course owned by the Resistance. Due to the city's layout, Resistance agents are the only residents who know how to drive since no one who lives and stays in Venezia has any need to operate a car. Travel between islands has always been by boat, and the roads in Venezia are too narrow for anything but foot travel. This car is fancier than anything I've been allowed to handle, though.

The prince pulls out a map from the glove compartment that has the route highlighted for me. Given it's the only place he said he's allowed to go, it's likely the only map he's ever needed. "I'll give you directions, but it helps to have a visual," he says, setting the map in his lap. He tells me where to turn to get off the castle grounds, Franco following behind us in the other car. Once we're on the highway, the car grows silent, electricity buzzing in the small space.

This will be an awkward three-hour drive if I don't do something to break the silence. "So, what should I call you?" I ask him, cringing at the way it came out.

"What do you mean?" he asks.

"Well, don't expect me to curtsy and call you 'Your Highness' every time I address you," I state matter-of-factly.

"Good, I wouldn't want you to," he beams. Is he trying to be charming on purpose, or is that second nature for him? "Just call me Nic. That's what my brother used to call me."

"Okay, Nic," I say, trying to adjust myself to the informal nickname. "Since we're going to be spending more time together than I initially realized, I should probably tell you my real name." I brace myself for whatever reaction my confession brings, anger or hurt being the two obvious emotions. Instead, Nic chuckles.

"I should have known you'd told me a fake name from the moment I saw you were going to use me as target practice. Tell me then, what is your real name?"

It shouldn't have mattered to me whether he was upset, but I'm relieved to see that he's smiling. "Adelina, but people call me Lina."

"Adelina," he says to himself quietly to try my name out. Hearing his voice saying my real name sends shivers down my spine. I tell myself that whatever this chemistry is, it's one-sided. Traveling around with a runaway prince might get dangerous, and I can't lose focus by daydreaming about his blue eyes or imagining his lips on mine.

I let the silence take over again as I think through what I want to ask him. "You said your father doesn't go to the vacation home anymore," I start to phrase my question, "but why is that?"

Something in his demeanor changes, but I wait for his response. "It reminds him too much of my mother. The house belonged to her family and was passed down to her. When she was alive, we would go there twice a year as a family, but he hasn't set foot in that place since she passed away."

His mother, the queen, has been dead for almost fifteen years. I was young, but I still remember how people reacted when the news reached Venezia. Never before and never since have I seen such collective grieving. Even among the Resistance, she was beloved and known for her kindness. As Dario had told me, the queen was the only one who could temper the king's ruthlessness, and her death meant the death of hope for some. While her loss was a symbol of dark times to come, to Nic, the loss was far greater.

Though I didn't know her, my impressions of him so far suggest that he's much more like her than his father. The man sitting next to me had lost both his mother and his older brother less than five years apart. Never knowing my parents is its own kind of grieving, but it's different than his grief since I never knew them to realize how much I've missed out. In his case, he knows the loss.

"I never knew either of my birth parents," I share with him to match the vulnerability he's showing me. "I was adopted as a baby. I don't even know their names or who they were or if they're still alive."

"It must be difficult not knowing," he says with a small appreciative smile. His words hang in the air as I check my mirrors to ensure Franco is still following behind us.

"Did you enjoy your birthday party?" I ask him to make small talk, hoping it will lighten the mood.

Nic has a concentrated expression when he replies, "It felt like what life must have been for a young female in the 1800s being introduced to society for her first season." My look of confusion spurs him on. "After being secluded during my formative years, I'm thrust into a ball in my honor where men are expected to ask women to dance, and women are expected to be dressed up and demure. Fathers are there to garner favor with the king, mothers are there to marry their children off, and the men my age that I grew up with are doing what they can to avoid the determined mothers. I didn't realize that being a noble meant socialization was still that antiquated."

I hadn't thought of it that way when I walked into the extravagant ballroom. The crystal chandeliers and stained glass windows gave the illusion that I'd just stepped foot into a fairytale. When I slipped on the scarlet gown that had been precisely tailored to flatter my figure while also concealing a few weapons, I saw a stranger in the mirror's reflection, a girl who could pass for a princess.

What seemed antiquated to him was straight from a storybook to me, right down from the moment my heel had caught on my hem and I crashed into a handsome prince. Had I been any other girl, perhaps a nobleman's daughter, I'd be able to tell people that the moment he helped me up was love at first sight rather than the moment I'd come face to face with the man I'd been trained to kill. I intended to get a good enough look to verify I was aiming at the right person later that night. Instead, I'm driving his Maserati to a villa in Napoli in the middle of the night. Franco and I are supposed to be heading south either way, making this only a slight detour.

"I think it's kind of nice to see people dressed up in beautiful clothes to celebrate something or someone," I admit to him. "There are so many reasons for people to be sad or angry, but we need more celebrations. Celebrations remind people that we have something to hope for."

"And do you feel more hopeful with what you've seen of me so far?" he asks bashfully.

"You wouldn't be alive if I didn't," I say bluntly.

An hour into the drive, I'm grateful that Franco insisted that I sleep and rest during the day. It made sense to conserve my energy for the ball and aftermath, and that was before the prospect of a three-hour drive lay ahead of me. I quickly glance over to see Nic with his head resting against the window and his eyes closed. When he had planned to drive himself tonight, he must not have calculated how draining a large party would be on his energy levels. After a while, it was overwhelming to me, and I wasn't the focal point of the night. I also have more social practice than he's used to in that castle. Until I saw his sleeping figure, I hadn't noticed just how much of a burden he carries when awake and conscious. He looks more boy than man without the future responsibilities of the kingdom hovering in his mind.

At the beginning of the third hour, Nic stirs and yawns as he wakes up from his nap. "Do you need me to take over driving, or are you good to finish out the last leg?" he asks with sleep still in his voice. The sound of it is so adorable that I grip the steering wheel to keep myself from melting.

"I've had longer, more strenuous days than today," I reply with a shrug. It isn't a lie, given the training I've endured. On more than one occasion, the Resistance sent me with a regiment into the Dolomites for a week. The last day of the excursion was always one in which we traveled on foot for 24 hours without rest. My solace then and my solace now is that a bed awaits me at the end.

He says, "I don't doubt that. I can't imagine that the Resistance would have sent just anyone to assassinate a prince. In fact, I expected the attempt."

"You didn't seem very surprised when you talked to me, even though I'm sure I hadn't given away my location or presence." It had taken me by surprise when he spoke out loud to me as if I weren't quiet or well hidden in the darkness.

"Either you or one of the staff left my chamber door cracked open," he reveals. "Plus, I would have to be very ignorant not to anticipate a possible target on my back. I'm very aware of how much my father is despised. I'd want to kill myself too if I thought there was a chance I would be like him or worse."

Unable to give an appropriate response, I settle into the calmness of the night. For the duration of the drive, Nic only speaks up to direct me. The quietness isn't uncomfortable, though, with no pressure to keep a conversation going. After the last turn, I can see the dark villa at the end of a long drive, illuminated only by the car headlights. He points out where I should park, and Franco follows our lead.

"Wait, let me get the door for you," he says as he rushes into the night air and around the car to open the door for me like he had when we started the journey. Out of the corner of my eye, I can see Franco stretching his legs and smirking at the prince's gesture. The muscles in my legs are tight as Nic offers his hand to pull me out of the car. I internally lecture myself about not taking the time to stretch before the drive, but just the movement loosens my muscles. We allow Nic to take the lead to unlock the entrance to the villa.

"There's no one else here," Franco confirms. "We're the only cars, and this is too far out for anyone to walk or take public transportation. If this were a trap, there would be at least one car here for someone to escape. I'll do a perimeter search to confirm, but the prince has been honest with us so far, it seems." I thank him as we walk inside the now-lit villa. Nic leads us to the kitchen and pours us two glasses of water from a bottle in the fridge.

"I asked someone to stock the fridge in case I decided to stay for more than a day before leaving," he explains, opening the cupboards to take inventory on the food supply. "Let me show you to your rooms."

He leads us up a set of stairs to a hallway, turning on lights as we go. Though it's certainly no castle, the villa is well-taken care of and owned by a wealthy family. There are four bedrooms on this level for the three of us, with mine on one side of the hallway, while Franco and Nic claim the two on the opposite side. "Yours has the best view," Nic whispers to me before he and Franco go back out to the cars to bring in our luggage. At their insistence, I wait at the doorway to my room, the tiredness overtaking my need for independence.

"You're safe to rest," Franco reassures me as he hands me my suitcase a few minutes later. "You need it after everything today. I'll keep an eye on the prince."

I plop down on the bed with the intent of taking a light sleep, only to open my eyes again hours later. Golden streams of sunlight filter through the cracks between the curtains as my mind digs through my memories from the past twenty-four hours to figure out where I am. I notice a blanket draped over me, something I don't remember doing myself. When I hear the quiet knock at my door, I croak, "Come in." In a flash, I worry about my appearance, but it's too late to stop whoever is at the door.

Nic, appearing well-rested and freshly showered, comes in holding a tray of food. His hair is still damp, and I'm slightly envious of how clean he must feel. If my stomach weren't growling at the smell of the breakfast he brings me, I would shower before eating. The croissants appear warm and flaky.

"Franco told me that you prefer cappuccinos in the morning," Nic says, handing me the cup of espresso with steamed and frothed milk. It's endearing seeing someone who usually has a whole staff of people who do things like this for him make my coffee without my having to ask. "We have a fancy espresso machine in the kitchen."

I'm too busy enjoying the flavors of my plate to hold much of a conversation, and he slips out and back to the hallway. I eat my breakfast in privacy and take a shower before bringing the dirty dishes to the kitchen. Franco and Nic are in the dining room, all tensions from the night before gone. "I'm sort of jealous she got to drive your car," I hear Franco's voice say as I turn toward the kitchen.

"Lina, let me get that for you," Nic hurries to me to take the dishes from my hands. Frozen, I watch as he washes the cup and plate in the sink and dries them with a towel. He had said that they don't have staff here at the villa, but it hadn't occurred to me that it also meant that when he comes here, he does everything for himself like a normal person. Most go on vacation to escape everyday responsibilities, but he comes here for a different set of them.

"It's safe here," Franco says to me for the second time since arriving, and I remember his promise to perimeter the premises. I was so drained that I hadn't even waited for his confirmation before passing out. At least we don't need to rush out of here anytime soon. We have a few days before we're expected to report to our allies in the first town on our return route. Right now is when we're supposed to be lying low and avoiding suspicion.

"When you're both ready, I'll give a tour of the villa grounds," Nic interrupts, his blue eyes brighter in the natural daylight that fills the room from the open curtains. I discreetly inspect this man who has opened up his vacation home and trusted two strangers who tried to kill him last night. His eyes hold no visible signs of suspicion, only excitement. Unsuccessfully, I tell myself that his eagerness is less about me and more about his having extended interaction with others his age. I wonder what kind of mental or emotional abuse his father's actions have wrought on his only remaining son, whether the king intended it that way or not.

No longer cloaked by the darkness of night, I can see that the house is much larger than I had originally assumed a few hours ago. Nic leads us to the main entrance and hall, where a marble staircase ascends to the mezzanine level on which the three of us slept the night before. The main level also includes a study, a full kitchen, a formal dining room, a mudroom, and a drawing room. He points out the back staircase, the one we must have used last night from the kitchen.

As if that weren't enough space, he takes us up to the top level where six more master suites lie untouched. The upper level has another smaller kitchen. It's as if the house had been built for several families to go on vacation together. Franco and I follow him down the stairs to the bottom level and through an entrance to an indoor pool, sauna, and gym. Outside, the gardens come alive with shades of green as the light reflects off the water of the outdoor pool. All of this is too much for one person alone. The villa may not have staff currently, but based on the servants' quarters, it had in the past. My mind tries to conjure up the types of people who would have stayed here, but it draws a blank.

I eye the pool longingly, knowing that the afternoon will be the prime time to enjoy the water. Swimming is another required skill for Resistance trainees, but most city residents have also learned at some point. Though the main island doesn't have any beaches, one would only need a boat to find a beach among the numerous islands of the lagoon. The adventures to be had in that area alone seem endless.

Noticing my gaze, Nic says, "Let me check the water to ensure the levels are good. Whoever stocked the fridge probably tested the water and made any adjustments, but I want to be sure before any of us use it. It should be ready to go after lunch."

Franco and I go back inside the house, leaving Nic to add salt to the pool water I admired. "Dario is going to be very jealous when we get home and I tell him about this place," Franco says, smiling and shaking his head. "It gives a whole new meaning to 'sparing no expense' when I see a villa like this that's unoccupied for the most part."

"I would probably get lost if he hadn't given us a tour before I wandered off on my own," I say in agreement.

"You seemed to be able to find your way around the castle just fine, which is impressive given it's the only time you've been there," Nic says behind me, drying his hands on his shirt like he isn't royalty.

I guessed what Franco was going to say next before it came out of his mouth. "That's because she's been studying maps and blueprints of the castle since she was sixteen." Well, Franco must trust him to have spilled that secret tidbit.

"How intense is the training that you've had to go through?" Nic asks, gesturing for us to follow him into the study. I step in to take a better look at the room he had pointed out to us earlier this morning, memorizing details for when I tell Maria about this later.

Maria. Home. The possibility of returning isn't a dream anymore, but a very probable destination. By not following through, I'd avoided the immediate danger while opening the door to more uncertainties. Beyond making it to the villa, we haven't discussed details of the checkpoints that lie ahead or how long Nic intends to travel with us. Beneath the surface excuse of wanting to escape his father, if only temporarily, my gut speculates there's another reason he was desperate to leave the castle. I don't push him to tell us, though, letting him open up whenever he chooses to. If he wants our help, he won't keep secrets from us.

"Six days a week with one day off, holidays are no exception," I answer.

Nic whistles and says, "Sounds tough, but at least you get a day off. There's no day off from being the crown prince." Not even running away from home changes who he's supposed to be.

"Is this you?" I ask Nic, pointing to a boy in a painting with the same blue eyes but with blond hair. He must have been around five or six in that captured frame of time.

"Isn't it crazy how light my hair used to be?" he grins, pointing at his now dark brown hair. "Both my parents had dark hair, so my light hair was a surprise. It was within a year of that painting that it started to darken." Genetics always interests me in how the physical traits of two people combine in one child who resembles both father and mother. I would speculate whether my curls were the same as my mom's texture and whether my dad had the same dark chocolate eyes. One of the advantages of nobility is that they have paintings and portraits passed down through the generations to show the passing of such genes.

"This is one of my favorite books," Franco says as he flips through the pages of a green hardback he's pulled off one of the bookshelves. I picture Nic in the armchair by the fireplace with a book in his hands, indulging himself on the collections that line the shelved walls. Someone like him must be an avid reader with the time he's spent away from the distractions of people and everyday life.

Nic opens the cupboards on the bottom and pulls out what appears to be a journal with a yellow cover. "Part of why I wanted to come here and stay for a few days before leaving is that my mother's old journals are all stored here," he explains, opening the aged pages before closing the cover. "I'm searching for information that my father may have been trying to hide from me. She might have written something down in her journals that could be useful." He puts the one he checked back into the cupboard and pulls out another with a light blue cover.

The prince's statement has intrigued Franco, and he offers his help on the search. While the idea of reading through the deceased queen's thoughts is appealing to my love for puzzle-solving, I can feel my hunger urging me back to the kitchen. One of us has to prepare lunch, and I'm the only willing volunteer.

"What are we looking for?" Franco asks him as I exit the room.

"Someone with the surname Sozzini," Nic replies. I can't recall when and where, but the name sounds familiar to me.

THE WATER BECKONS me like a siren call, and I go willingly. Although it seemed improbable that I would need a swimsuit, I was instructed to pack for every possible scenario. Espionage on a beach is a widely coveted Resistance mission. I change into the striped one-piece, cute and practical, and look out my window to make sure the pool hasn't disappeared on me like a mirage. The surface glistens in the light's reflection.

Saltwater surrounds my hair, my feet, my every inch of skin when I dive in the deeper end. For a split second, I'm just a girl once again, playing with my sister as we pretend to be mermaids. I glide through the water as if it were second nature to me. I swim a few laps, switching strokes to give my muscles work at every angle. I'm so consumed by the enjoyment of being in a pool for fun that I miss when Nic walks out of the villa wearing his swimming trunks and holding two towels. I stop at the end where he stands watching me.

"Are you going to come in, or did you take your shirt off just to show off?" I tease, but then blush when I realize what I said. Shirtless, muscular men are a regular part of my training regimen. This is far from unusual, yet I feel like a teenage girl noticing the male body for the first time. I'd felt his strength when he pulled me off the floor last night and when he'd danced with me, but feeling and seeing are two different experiences. He is a work of art with the toned lines of his biceps, pectorals, and abdominals, lines that make me wish I were artistic enough to sketch. He jumps in the pool close enough to me to splash me with water. That is his way of answering my question.

When his head comes back up through the water, he turns to me in a mock shrug. I attempt to chase him down to somehow make him pay, but he swims away, just out of reach. There's splashing and some playful glares back and forth until we're both exhausted. He helps me out of the water, and we sit on loungers on the side, letting the sunshine dry us off.

"I'm trying to figure out how many different ways you could probably kill me," Nic says nonchalantly as if we were discussing gelato flavors and not methods of murder, specifically his.

"There are a limited number of ways to kill someone," I muse despite my discomfort at the topic. It had only been yesterday that we met, yet the image of his lifeless body would be a nightmare. "Poison, arson, drowning, strangulation, stabbing, impalement–"

"Wouldn't poisoning me have been an easier and cleaner means of assassination?" he asks. "I mean, you could have easily slipped something into my drink or food."

He makes a solid point, so I run the scenario through in my head. "A poison that works too quickly in a room full of potential witnesses would arouse suspicion, making that a riskier venture than the original bow-and-arrow plan. It would have to be a slow-acting poison, and even then, the message may not express the same way. With poison, any one of the hundreds of guests could have been at fault, rather than it being a clear sign of the Resistance. If the poison is too slow, someone could also find an antidote. Too many factors."

"Setting fire to a stone castle isn't a good plan either," he surmises. "Strangulation would also be difficult given that, despite your training and speed, I have mass and strength at my advantage. The hardest part would be to find a way to defend myself without accidentally hurting you."

"Who would be next in line to the throne in that hypothetical situation?" It's a question I should have asked before now.

"Considering the bow and arrow in your hands last night, it's not so hypothetical. I have distant cousins who could be traced back to the royal line," he thinks out loud. "My father could also remarry and try to have another heir. It's how I can tell how much he loved my mother—he hasn't remarried even though it's been nearly fifteen years since she died. Anytime I find myself wondering if he's capable of love, I remind myself of the man he once was. He's certainly not too old to find another wife, though I cringe at the prospect that he might marry someone close to my age for reproduction purposes." I also shudder at the idea of someone my age being married to the king. With the prince of marrying age, it would almost make more sense to try for a grandson.

I glance at Nic, his body leaning back and eyes closed as he soaks in the warmth of the late afternoon sun. As if his title alone doesn't make his possibilities endless, he is beautiful. The shape of his face, the color of his eyes, and the parts of his body that I can see as he relaxes in his swimming trunks are reason enough. If he lived in Venezia, the same girls who followed Dario around would ogle at Nic, too.

It would be easier for me if he were like his father; I wouldn't need to fight these newfound feelings and attractions. Without the interference of the Resistance, someone in his position would be back at the castle, making plans on which girl from the party to check in on. Instead, he's here with me rather than someone who could realistically be a future queen. If he were like his father, he wouldn't be here at all. I don't know whether his being alive is safer or more dangerous for me.

Before I let the hopelessness of our connection overtake my enjoyment of this precious time, I stand up from my chair and wrap the towel he brought out for me around my body. "I'm gonna go inside and change into some dry clothes," I tell him as I walk back toward the house for much-needed distance from his intoxicating presence.

CHAPTER 4

Niccolò

I'm disappointed to see her leave and also relieved to have a moment to collect my thoughts. It's hard to focus on my reason for coming here–to find information about my betrothed–when Lina is anywhere in my vicinity. The attraction I feel toward her is like a magnet that's impossible to pull away from. I wait long enough to be sure she's in her room before I go back inside, spotting Franco on my way to my room.

"Hey, you missed out on the pool today," I say to him, more to be polite than anything else. I'm somewhat appreciative of the alone time I'd had with Lina.

"Oh, I didn't miss anything," Franco replies cryptically without moving his eyes from the book in his hands. I notice the windows on the side of the room facing the pool are open. Maybe those moments weren't so private after all. He is here as her partner on this mission, so I can't fault him for that.

Ten minutes later, I've changed into casual clothes and look at the ingredients in the kitchen to ensure I have what I need for the recipe I chose for dinner. I'm pulling items from the shelves and fridge when Lina sneaks in silently. I jump at the surprise, even if she didn't intend to scare me. She must be so well trained that it's become natural for her to move noiselessly.

Seeing my jolted reaction, Lina gives me an apologetic expression. "I forget how quiet I am. My family is accustomed to it, so I didn't consider its effect on you. Is there anything I can do to help?"

I assign her to be in charge of the sauce before asking, "What is your family like? You already know so much about mine." I might as well have asked, *What is it like to be normal?*

"I'm adopted and don't know anything about my biological family," she says as she minces the garlic. "The family I live with has a daughter who is practically my sister and close enough to my age that we were in classes together at school for a while. She and I still share a bedroom even though I could have moved out years ago. Just before I left, she and my main training partner got engaged."

"Are you happy for them?" I ask after picking up on a hint of sadness in her last statement.

"Of course I am!" she insists emphatically. "They're the two most important people in my life, and now they get to build a future together. They are the type of couple you see together and think, 'Wow, they're perfect for each other.' I've just been worried that I won't live long enough to see them get married. Or that if I do, I won't find something remotely close to what they have together. But if you tell anyone I admitted that, I'll have to kill you."

Her hesitancy about her future troubles me. If my well-thought-out plan to make my father believe I am staying at the villa for the next few weeks doesn't work and we are caught, her fears would be justifiable. Even in the long term, she's part of the group against the throne I'm to inherit. For right now, they trust me as much as I trust them to help me disappear without leaving a trace behind. For the foreseeable future, our odds of survival are intertwined, relying on the others' abilities.

In addition, her doubts about finding love irk me. She isn't the one legally bound to marry a girl whose whereabouts are unknown. I can't even entertain the thought of a life with someone else until I get the answers I'm searching for. As soon as she's returned home, Lina is free to open up her heart to anyone she fancies and have a somewhat normal life without the looming expectancy to produce an heir. I haven't even considered what I'll do once I find the elusive information. Locating the Sozzini girl seems like the obvious next step if I do find proof that she's alive.

While we eat dinner, Franco goes over the plan for the next city, Lucera. The drive will be about the same distance as the castle to the villa, but with only one car, since I will be leaving my Maserati here.

"How were you planning on leaving the villa with your original plan?" Lina asks me. It had been the hardest puzzle for me to figure out back when I thought I'd be coming here alone. As far as the general public was concerned, I would be mostly safe if I didn't draw attention to myself since most of the Kingdom hadn't seen me recently enough to know what I look like now. The biggest problem would be the identification papers required to use public transportation, such as the train. Fortunately, I found someone willing to procure a fake ID for me and leave it here at the villa for me to retrieve.

"Fake ID," I say as if the answer were obvious. The two trained agents exchange indecipherable looks. I wait uncomfortably for either one of them to respond.

"That probably would have worked, at least for a couple of weeks," Franco concedes with a shrug. "But as soon as your father realized you had run away, the train or bus station would become the first place you'd be caught. Public transportation is the first to increase surveillance in that type of situation." He isn't telling me something I wasn't already aware of. I had just been hoping that the time I did get as a head start would be enough.

"Where would you stay?" Lina asked, the more curious of the two of them. Franco and Lina have an itinerary that likely involves checkpoints with Resistance allies. They need to remain as much under the radar as possible, especially if a dead prince had been discovered in his chamber. A living runaway prince isn't much better.

One of the advantages of my position is having access to more money than I or my father knows what to do with. "Secluded inns, paying with cash, tipping for discretion," I list off. "Believe it or not, I'm fairly good at reading people and whether or not they're likely to help me. I'm resourceful."

They both seem satisfied with my answer, as if they needed to be sure I would have survived without their help. We finish eating, and Franco offers to wash the dishes since he's the only one who didn't contribute to making the meal. I oblige, eager to return to the study where my mother's journals await.

Alone in the quiet room, I scan page after page, sometimes pausing to read the sections where she writes about my father. She used language such as "hopelessly in love" and "pull of destiny" to describe the early days of her relationship with him. Wanting to compare it to his thoughts on the matter, I pull out the box where my mother had stored the letters he used to write to her. The romantic words are undoubtedly his handwriting, but the tenderness behind them doesn't seem to fit the cold and calculating man he has been for most of my recent years. As I read, I speculate whether this version of my parents would have let circumstances such as a betrothal or title keep them from finding a way to be together.

I close that journal and open another one with dates closer to my birth date. The first few entries are mostly about my older brother and how fast he was growing. The entries are chronological, with my birth occurring somewhere in the middle. In my mind, I can picture her glowing with pride over her two sons. On one of the pages toward the middle, my eyes catch mention of the name Valentina.

> *The weather today proved to be perfect for spending time outdoors. My lady-in-waiting packed a picnic basket and helped me corral the boys to the gazebo on the east end of the grounds. Valentina joined me there for lunch, desperate to get out of the house with her husband away on a business trip. She and Alessandro have been trying for a baby for nearly two years now, and she tried to hide how upset she was that it was unsuccessful again this month. I still remember the days when she and I were both engaged to be married to our husbands, making lofty plans of at least one love match between our children to join our families. Once I'd given birth to a second son, Vincenzo finally agreed to the idea of a betrothal for our younger son, Niccolò. I can only hope that Valentina's expectations flourish. It's hard watching my dearest friend struggle with barrenness while I've been blessed to have two strong boys.*

My mother and Valentina Sozzini had been close friends. If she had ever mentioned it to me before she died, I was too young to remember. This is a clue and a step in the right direction, though. The betrothal wasn't meant to be a political move, but rather a joining of two families who cared for each other. The disappearance of the House of Sozzini would have affected my mother, and if anyone knew what happened, it would have been her. I scour the next few pages for mention of her friend again until I stop at the second-to-last page.

> *Today has been a monumental day for both the House of Mattei and the House of Sozzini. Last week, when Valentina shared with me that she was finally expecting a child, I insisted that we make the betrothal official as a sign of trust that her baby would be a healthy daughter. If their child is a son and she never conceives a daughter, the contract would become irrelevant and void. Vincenzo relented, and today the document was signed and sealed. While I've worried in the past that Niccolò may not take well to the arranged marriage when he comes of age, the innocence in his blue eyes reassures me. My younger son is already so much like me that I find it impossible that he won't love a daughter of Alessandro and Valentina. Their daughter would be their heir, and Niccolò could marry into land of his own without being forced to live under the shadow of Carlo, who is first in line to be king.*

It's almost as if I can hear her voice in my head as I read the words she scribed. My mother didn't write these journals for herself; she wrote them for me, maybe even for Carlo. Whether or not she suspected she could die before I was old enough to understand, she wrote this down anyway and left the journals in a place she knew I would come back to. If my father were aware that her journals are still here, he would have gotten rid of them like he'd erased most records of the Sozzinis from the castle library. He was and is too busy being king to notice his wife was leaving behind traces of the truth. While this information is helpful, it still isn't the answer I need now.

There's a gentle knock at the door, and Lina walks in, carrying two steaming cups. "You like macchiatos, right?" she asks me as she hands me the warm cup of espresso and milk foam. I set it down at the side table nearest me and clear the seat next to me for her. She notes my gesture and sits on the other side of the loveseat, her coffee in hand.

"I'll let it slide this time, but you should know that it's against cultural rules to drink coffee with milk after breakfast," I banter before taking a sip of my favorite way to drink espresso. "There's grappa in the wine cellar for caffè corretto." Internally, I am grateful that she hadn't added alcohol to my coffee. Her scent alone is enough to intoxicate me.

She sticks out her tongue at me. "This is one rule that was made to be broken. If I want milk in my espresso, I should be able to have it at any time of the day I choose." There is no arguing with her logic there. I have no objections to any form of caffeine when I still have so much to search. Needing a mind rest, I savor the flavor of the coffee. Lina does the same with her own, giving small hums of approval with each sip.

"Do the safe-houses come with coffee, or is that something we'll have to risk going into town to find?" I ask her when my cup is empty, breaking the comfortable silence that had settled over the room.

"Don't remind me," she groans, giving me the only

explanation I need. "Although they may have moka pots. The other advantage of going into town, though, is for gelato."

I add gelato to the mental catalogue of things that Lina likes, convincing myself that keeping track is merely a friendly gesture. She had spared my life, after all. The least I can do is buy her ice cream. Forcing myself to get back on track, I stand and return the journal I'd just read to the shelf and pull the next one off the shelf.

When I turn around, Lina is right behind me as if she's trying to get a good look at the collection of diaries. She's so close that I can feel her warmth radiating from her skin and smell the lingering salt in her hair from our swim in the pool this afternoon. My eyes catch the way she flickers her gaze between my eyes and my mouth, and I can read her wordless request. It's the same longing I've felt every minute I've spent around her. As her lips slowly grow closer, the hunger in me goes frantic, at war with the conscience reminding me of why I can't. If I start this, I'm not sure if I can ever stop, and that would only lead to broken hearts and broken promises.

"Lina, I can't," I barely manage to whisper before I muster enough willpower to create a few feet of distance between our bodies. My breathing is heavy as if I had gone for a run, and, in a sense, I had. She looks dejected by my refusal, an expression that causes me physical pain to see on her face. I try to explain, "I said I can't, not that I don't want to."

"Right, because you're a prince while I'm an assumed orphan who works for the organization formed in opposition to your father's rule," she says with a sigh as she plops on the loveseat again. Aside from when she fell at the ball last night, that plop is the sole ungraceful movement I have seen from her.

Against my better judgment to get close to her again, I sit on the other side of the loveseat and hold her hands in mine. "Lina," I start, but then pause to think about my words. "Yes, those circumstances aren't exactly favorable when you're talking about a lifetime together. There's something else, though–the ultimate reason why I wanted to leave the castle. Not too long ago, I discovered that my parents had entered into a legally binding betrothal agreement, promising me to marry the daughter of another noble family. My father had never mentioned the engagement to me, and given how little I could find about her or her family, I have reason to believe he hid it. I don't even know if she's still alive, but until I find her, I can't let myself fall for someone else. It wouldn't be fair to any of us."

Her stillness worries me, but she hasn't jerked her hands away from mine either. Patiently, I wait for her reaction, growing nervous with each passing second. Finally, she says, "If it's something your father doesn't want found, I can almost guarantee that the Resistance has evidence stored somewhere." It confirms the thought I hadn't let myself hope in because the possibility of it hadn't been probable until I met her. She gently pulls her hands away from mine. "I should wash these cups out and get ready for bed." I don't stop her or call after her. I fill my hands again with the pages of my mother's handwriting and continue my search.

A folded piece of paper falls out of the middle of this book, piquing my curiosity. The note is written in code, but I recognize the pattern as one my mother and I had invented when I was a boy. Decoding the message is long and tedious, but whatever truth it contained must be dangerous and intended for me. Half an hour later, I soak in the weighty news, reading it several times to ensure it's correct.

My son, I fear your father's actions may have cost you someone dear. If you haven't uncovered it yet, you are betrothed to be married by a contract

Zeta Verde. I say the name out loud until I'm certain I'll never forget it. Then, I throw the note into the fireplace on the small chance that my father comes here later to search for me. I put out the fire once I'm satisfied with the ashes it's left behind. With the journal that had hidden the note secure in my hand, I retreat to my bedroom to sleep for the night.

Sleep eludes me as my mind races to create a plan of action. Rather than finding an answer, I'd found another clue along the scavenger hunt. Discovering leads on Zeta Verde is unlikely at the castle or here at the villa, though, so nothing has changed. I will continue this journey with Lina and Franco and hope that my resolve lasts longer than the trek back to the Resistance. It has only been twenty-four hours, and I came unnervingly close to complicating the situation.

My betrothed is possibly in another country, potentially waiting for me to locate her, and I almost kissed a girl who lied about her name when we met with intentions to kill me. I need to have better control over myself if I am to fulfill my mother's wishes.

I WAKE the next morning with renewed determination. Any leftover frustrations I have due to unresolved desires can be worked out on the gym's equipment. After changing into gym shorts and a t-shirt, I chug a glass of water and rush to my salvation. Lina is already making her rounds on the weight-lifting machines, and if I'd had to guess, she has been working out for at least half an hour already.

"Do you normally get up this early to exercise?" I ask her as I do some warm-up stretches.

"I've never had two days in a row off from training since I was sixteen," she says in explanation. I don't miss the *never* part of her statement. It confirms that holidays aren't an exception to the schedule. I also don't miss her tone of voice, normal without hints of hurt or malice. She may be here for the same reason I am, but I am relieved that she isn't taking it out on me. Finally, I let out a breath I didn't know I had been holding. I add extra weight than usual to the machine before warming up. I'm ten minutes into my reps when she leaves after offering to make breakfast once she's changed clothes. Everything between us will stay friendly.

Franco has a half-asleep demeanor as he sips his coffee at the dining room table. My stomach growls when the smells wafting in the air hit my nostrils, causing my mouth to water. I nearly sprint up the stairs to shower, hoping that breakfast will be ready by the time I'm finished. There is something satisfying about knowing I've uncovered everything there is to be found here. We aren't leaving until tomorrow, which still gives me today to enjoy being here.

The brioche Lina baked is the perfect companion to my macchiato. Franco already looks more human than he did fifteen minutes ago, coming more alive with every bite of the bread. The beautiful woman made homemade bread.

"How did you find time to make this?" I ask as soon as the thought hits me. From experience, the dough needs two different times to rise before baking.

"I couldn't sleep last night, so I prepared the dough," she says nonchalantly. At least I wasn't the only one plagued with restlessness. When I had gone upstairs last night, I must have been too absorbed in my discovery to notice she was in the kitchen.

Finally functioning, Franco asks, "How late did you two stay up last night? After keeping watch our first night here after the ball, I could hardly keep my eyes open."

Lina and I briefly make eye contact before looking away. "I'm not sure how late Lina went to sleep," I hedge carefully, "but I found a secret note my mother had left behind for me." Lina's reaction to the news is one of ambivalent interest. After spending part of the day helping me search yesterday, Franco seems more excited to have a breakthrough in the mystery.

"Well, first I found out that my mom was close friends with Valentina Sozzini," I continue. "The betrothal was their idea, two young moms matchmaking their children by legal encouragement. The note went into more detail. Based on her words, my mother and the Sozzinis thought they and their daughter were in danger because of something to do with my father. They fled the country and initially planned to come back, but given how my father has only grown worse with losing his wife and eldest son, I believe they're still taking refuge in another country. My mother requested that I find them and gave me the name of Valentina's cousin, who may know where they are."

"Great, another name to track down," Lina says sarcastically, but I can tell it's lighthearted by the smile that follows.

"Zeta Verde," I tell them both, confident that they'll keep the secret. Franco and Lina have identical reactions of surprise and shock. When neither is forthcoming, I ask, "You both know who that is, don't you?"

"Director Verde," Lina whispers first, followed by Franco's nod of confirmation. It's the first I've heard them use the name, but by the title and the fact that they both know her, I would guess that she's an important authority figure in the Resistance. Who better to help a noble family flee the country than someone who already had allies and connections throughout the Kingdom, and who better to help the Sozzinis than someone who saw my father as an enemy? Perhaps their situation was the catalyst for the formation of one unified group. The very Resistance that had sent Lina to kill me holds the key to solving my quandary.

Franco says to Lina, "Looks like he's coming home with us."

"He's a prince, not a puppy," she muses. "He can come, but we can't keep him." Though I know her words hold deeper meaning than Franco would understand, I catch the unspoken hint. Once they have taken me to Zeta Verde, we will be saying goodbye forever. I will be on my own at that point. I give her a slight nod of agreement.

"If you found what you came here for, does that mean you have the day free before we head to the next stop tomorrow?" Franco asks. Lina has a knowing look as if she sees where his question leads. I nod as nervousness creeps in. "I think it's about time we test this prince's fighting skills. I need a sparring partner, and Lina isn't known to fight fair. Plus, I like it when my opponent is unpredictable."

Being secluded from society doesn't mean that I haven't had access to the finest tutors in the realm. While some days focused on learning laws and lineages, others were spent learning combat. I don't have the advanced level of training that my two companions share, but I certainly am not a novice. Franco seems more bemused by my level of skill than Lina. She observes us as if she expected I wouldn't fall flat on my face. Still, I'm willing to learn more from them, especially since there's a likelihood that I'll be alone in my search at some point in the future. Neither of them objects to my going to the Resistance with them, but I wonder what my being alive will mean for Lina. I have no way of knowing how they treat an agent who doesn't follow through on a mission.

By lunchtime, my body is ready to be done. I could have skipped the workout before breakfast and still gotten sufficient exercise by training with them. They must have incredible stamina to do that all day, six days a week. I tell them as much when we eat lunch together.

"Not all of us have Lina's crazy schedule," Franco laughs. "I get holidays off. It's Dario who's stuck with her most of the time." Right, Dario and Maria are her best friends. Surely their schedule will lighten up a bit when she returns. At least, she might get a longer break when her friends get married. No one can expect a groom to go straight back to work after marrying the love of his life. If I were in his place, being wed to someone I adore, I would need at least two weeks alone with her all to myself. I stop my imagination before it conjures up images of Lina again. I need this to get easier with time and familiarity.

"The hardest part about it is starting," Lina says with a shrug. "After a few weeks, your body adjusts. I'm so accustomed to it that I feel sluggish if I don't move around enough. Being in a car for three hours tomorrow might feel like torture."

I have the opposite feelings about tomorrow's stretch of the journey. Except for our middle-of-the-night breakaway from the castle, I haven't been a passenger in a car for a road trip since my brother died. Every other time I've come here since Carlo's death, I drove here alone. We are essentially stranding my car here tomorrow. At a later time, I will need a way to return here to retrieve it if my father doesn't find a way first. This spontaneous trip of mine is growing increasingly complex with every turn.

During the afternoon, we take advantage of the pool again, with Franco joining in on the fun. Lina is a force to be reckoned with when we gang up on her. For a fleeting moment, I pretend I'm a regular guy with his friends on an afternoon off in the nice weather—temporary simplicity.

CHAPTER 5

Adelina

"We're taking the scenic route since we're heading out a little earlier than needed," Franco announces as we say goodbye to the royal family's villa. In our Resistance car with tinted windows, he navigates us right through the heart of the city so that we can at least catch a glimpse of the streets and landmarks we couldn't experience firsthand. Franco and I may have been fine for excursions into the city, but bringing Nic with us and walking around in the open would have been a risk given his mother's connection to this area. Besides, our stay here wasn't long enough to warrant leaving the villa for necessities, and we need to get far from here in case the king discovers our involvement.

Mount Vesuvius looms large in the landscape, a prominent reminder that at any moment, danger could erupt. The threat of eruption and destruction of ancient cities hasn't stopped the present metropolis from thriving in this volcanic region. In the same way, flooding hasn't deterred the inhabitants of Venezia. We live life and adjust.

Though I can't see, touch, or smell them up close, the ant-sized boats floating in the Gulf of Napoli give me a twinge of homesickness. This is the coastline on the opposite end of the Kingdom, but it is still familiar in the way the people embrace life by the water. There will be no stopping for pizza here, though I hope to come back in the future. After all, perhaps my life after our return includes traveling.

Using Vesuvius as a guide, I determine how far we are from the city based on its size in the rearview mirror. Ironically, the side of Napoli closer to Vesuvius and the other mountains is more densely populated with towns than the area where we had been staying. Our car is swallowed up in the valley of the Partenio Mountains during our drive east toward Foggia. As the larger mountains become a distant memory, I begin to look forward to our upcoming week in Lucera. In a way, this route home is the Resistance's way of giving me a long-overdue vacation.

This region holds a different kind of beauty than what I'm accustomed to, with the hues of greens and golds rather than the blues of reflective water. I lose count of the number of vineyards and villas I can see from the road. Franco relaxes in the driver's seat while Nic is directly behind me in the backseat, as mesmerized by the landscape as I am. Because of his position as a prince, his father should have been taking him on tours around the kingdom he will one day rule. Princes who stay locked up in castles can easily lose touch with what life is like for the people.

More often than I should, I turn to steal glances at the prince in my periphery. My lapse in judgment that night in the study didn't seem to leave any permanent damage to our fragile friendship. I replay the moment in my head, the way he looked at me, and the pain in his eyes when he moved away. Respecting his boundaries would be easier if he didn't reciprocate my attraction and feelings. It's another level of difficulty to know that he wants this too, but is bound by law to marry another woman. He never had a choice in the matter.

In these everyday moments, it's easy to forget that he's the heir to the throne. I forget that we're essentially on opposite sides of an undeclared war, though if he could choose, he might prefer the Resistance. Because so much of my focus has been on training, I never fully understood all the pieces of the chess match between the king and the Resistance. When Nic ascends to the throne, there's a chance that we'll be at peace again. King Vincenzo seems to be the main enemy, after all. I try to imagine that future, one in which I'm invited to special events at the castle. I'll attend with a significant other, and we'll be close acquaintances with Nic and his queen. Our children might play together if I have any. Given the importance of continuing the royal line, he certainly would have children. In that world—in that future —we could still be part of each other's lives, even if we aren't together.

The view outside our windows transforms again as the city of Foggia grows nearer on the road ahead. Not only is it a sign that Lucera is near, but it is also where we will meet up with the Resistance allies for lunch. Much like me, they are creatures of habit who often have lunch in the same restaurant every day. The Osteria Numero Dieci is a restaurant frequented by visitors from other parts of the kingdom, which will also make our presence there unsuspected.

My legs are itching to get out of the car and move around. Noticing my fidgeting, Nic asks, "Does this safe-house come with food already stocked, or will we have to buy our groceries at the market?" It is a question neither Franco nor I has the answer to. Beyond the questions of who, where, and how long, we don't have details regarding our accommodations. At lunch, we will be handed the keys to the small villa in Lucera and shown the location on a map. We won't know more until we get to the property. His question does remind me of one minor aspect we had failed to discuss.

"Nic, out of abundance of caution, I don't think we should tell them who you are," I say to him, though it's for both the guys in the car. "Just because they're allies of the Resistance doesn't mean they will take kindly to our traveling around with a prince who was supposed to be killed a few days ago. We can't be sure how detailed their instructions are. We can tell them that Director Verde sent two agents as backup due to the extra security at the ball." Truthfully, if I had gone through with the assassination, having two partners would have been more of a hassle.

"See, I knew it was a good idea to do combat training yesterday," Franco points out. "And if they don't buy that, we'll insist that he was a last-minute addition to the plan because you couldn't bear to be away from him for that long."

I freeze, unsure of how to respond to the comment. His expression and tone are hard to read. If he doesn't know anything concrete, he at least suspects. It is a good enough explanation.

We drive through the Piazza Camillo Benso di Cavour near the restaurant, searching for a place to park. I'm distracted by the fountain in the center, wondering if people ever throw coins in the pool and make a wish. Perhaps only certain fountains are considered to have magical properties. Because Venezia doesn't have streets for cars, none of the fountains serve as the center of a roundabout the way this one does. Without much help from me, Franco finds a spot, and we walk a short distance to the meeting place.

"Yellow hat, two o'clock," I whisper to Franco when I see the sign we were told to look for.

The rest of our party is already seated outside when we arrive, and the hostess rushes to bring another chair and a place setting for the extra person in our group. Gino and Violeta introduce themselves, and we do the same, except Nic uses the name Pasquale rather than his own. The couple is ten years younger than I expected, maybe in their forties.

"We weren't sure how many of you there would be," Violeta says in apology. "I don't think Verde was sure herself when she sent us the note confirming your expected arrival." If the same is true for our other contacts, very little lying will be required on our end. People may make the assumption, and we won't tell them otherwise. Though I didn't press for details on why she chose our checkpoints, I suspect it's to get our opinion on which locations would be best suited for a new Resistance base.

I find a version of my favorite menu item here as well, smiling to myself in victory. Dario may not be here with me, but I've beaten him once again. When the waiter walks away after taking our orders, Gino pulls out a map from his pocket and shows us the route to take from our current location to the villa they prepared for our stay. Violeta circles other places of interest on the map, including the grocery stores and restaurants. There are a few other sights to see if we get bored, but it's mostly a rural town. She hands us the keys before the waiter brings out our food.

The second part of our meeting is purely for pleasure as they share what life is like in Foggia. Franco keeps up the majority of the conversation on our end by telling stories of the crazy stunts he's pulled in Venezia. By my memory, those stunts when he was younger were how he was scouted for the academy. Nic is as intrigued by the stories as our guests are. With our food devoured and our bellies full, we part ways as Gino and Violeta send their best wishes for us and Director Verde.

"That was easier than I thought it would be," I say once we're inside the car and away from any listening ears.

"I wasn't sure what I should or shouldn't say since I'm supposed to be an agent from a city that I've never visited,"

Nic confesses. "Most of what I know is what I've learned from books and maps. Based on what you've both shared with me, it's no comparison to experiencing the real thing."

I attempt to put myself in his shoes, using a different city as an example. I've now seen the castle and been inside its walls, but before I had, everything I knew of it was two-dimensional. Two very different types of knowledge, indeed. "If we tell you more stories, do you think it could help?" I offer up my only solution to the dilemma. "We can be specific about landmarks and the layout to give you a visual."

"Anything is better than nothing," he says with a shrug.

We spend the half-hour drive to the villa in the nearby town of Lucera telling childhood stories. To Nic, I explain the canal system as best as I can, describing the waterways as blood vessels that give life to the city. Some branches are larger than others, and each has its unique path. Franco tells us about the time he got lost in a part of the city he wasn't familiar with and walked right off the street into the water. Not every street has bridges that span across the canals to the other side.

Compared to the villa we had come from, this one is modest. For starters, this one has no pools compared to the two at the royal home. It isn't run-down by any measure, but it certainly isn't resort-level luxury. Considering we are all basically fugitives, it is nicer than we should expect.

"Two bedrooms, Nic and I will share," Franco announces after making a sweep of the layout.

"Sounds good to me," Nic says while carrying in some of the luggage from the car. His tone seems neutral about the prospect, yet I suspect he has never shared a room with anyone before. His usual vacation spot has more bedrooms than we could ever need.

As they had the first time, both men insist on bringing in all the luggage without my help. This time, though, I don't have exhaustion from a long night, but rather a pestering restlessness from the drive here. Because mine is the first bag brought in, I use the bedroom where Nic had dropped it off and change into lighter clothing. I pass them on my way out the front door.

"Where are you going?" Franco asks me, recognizing the look in my eyes.

"On a walk," I answer curtly. "I might as well, since the two of you seem to have everything covered." Without another glance, I jog out the door and into the fresh air.

The familiar motion and distance from the men give me the time I need to process the current status of our mission. We prepared for the King's possible reactions to his son's assassination—either the news would spread as quickly as possible, or he would keep it under wraps as long as possible while discreetly hunting down the Resistance. His past actions suggested the latter would be more likely. Most of the Kingdom didn't learn of Prince Carlo's death until weeks after, and the Resistance only knew sooner because of our intel within the castle. If Director Verde knows that the prince is still alive, I assume she would have been at lunch today with our contacts for an immediate debriefing.

Although I have misgivings about following the original route and timing back to the Resistance headquarters, I still have doubts about trusting Nic. I can't dismiss the possibility that he's acting and plotting to betray us, but we can keep him from the Resistance headquarters long enough for his true colors to become evident. No one can pretend to be kind forever; however, I would like to pretend that the chemistry between us doesn't exist due to his betrothal.

By the time I return from my excursion of more running than walking, Nic has already written out a grocery list, and Franco has chosen a grocery store to go to. They both look at me expectantly as I drink a glass of water.

"The kitchen has the non-perishables we'll need, but we still have to go into town to get fresh ingredients," Nic explains to me. "I'll make dinner tonight, but feel free to add anything that you think we'll need." My eyes scan his comprehensive list, not spotting anything amiss. For someone who's likely never stepped foot inside a grocery store, he is at least good at this part of the venture.

"How do you know how to cook?" I ask Nic as I hand him back the list.

Satisfied that I have no additions, he smiles and replies, "When you're locked away from society for years, you have to keep yourself preoccupied somehow. There are plenty of staff who were willing to show me a thing or two. Plus, my mother taught me a few family recipes when we would stay at the villa." At least he isn't a prince without useful life skills.

"Let's get going," Franco says to us with the car keys in his hands. "I'm already getting hungry again, and you know I can't be trusted to follow a list at the grocery store. Lina, you have five minutes to change and get in the car." I beam at his challenge. Rushing to my room for the week, I kick off my shoes, rip my still-sweaty clothes off, and throw on the first thing I can find. Decent enough. I pull my hair out of the loose braid I'd had it in and shake out my curls for a few seconds. I reapply some deodorant and slip on my shoes in record time. On the way out the door, I grab the bags I'd thought to pack in case this occasion arose. Franco and Nic are both waiting in the car, the latter with his eyes on his watch.

After I'm in the front passenger seat with my seatbelt on, Nic says to Franco, "Four minutes and fifty-five seconds. That's impressive."

"Did you think all my training was hand-to-hand combat and archery?" I joke, but it is a learned skill.

"How do you think she changed from that red dress to her all-black outfit and got in the position of hiding in your chambers in such a short amount of time?" Franco brings up. I still wish I'd gotten to wear that dress for longer than a few hours.

The grocery store is a shorter drive away than I had anticipated, but I also hadn't glanced at the speedometer on the way. Franco drives fast on a normal basis; when food is involved, there's no telling what speed he's willing to risk. "I'll wait here," Franco says after he puts the car in park. "I can't be trusted not to buy the whole store if I go inside." He makes a solid argument, so Nic and I walk into the store together.

"Have you ever been inside one of these?" I ask him in a light tone as I hand him a coin to insert in the shopping cart.

"Actually, no," he replies sheepishly. "Seems I've been missing out on a lot."

I push the cart as he walks close to my side, quietly asking me about etiquette and rules. When we arrive at the fresh produce, I show him where the produce bags and single-use gloves are. Once we've picked up all the fruits and vegetables on his list, I show him how to use the scale by typing in the product number.

"It saves time at the checkout because it prints out a barcode for you with the price right here," I explain to him as we weigh the tomatoes. "Plus, if you're on a budget, it's helpful to have an idea of how much you're spending before you get to a register." Nic picks up on things quickly, and we're soon moving through the other aisles in search of eggs and milk.

An elderly lady is holding a basket in the milk aisle with a lost expression on her face. When she notices us, she asks, "Excuse me, young man, can you help me get that carton of milk on the top shelf there?" She points to the product she's referring to, and Nic gladly helps her, using his height to his advantage. I'm not quite tall enough to reach the top shelf as effortlessly as he can, but I usually find a way to grab what I need without assistance from another.

The lady smiles gratefully at him, then she turns her attention to me. "You'd better make sure you hold onto that one. He's one of the good ones." Before I can respond, she walks away toward the checkout. Though Nic is close enough to have overheard her statement, he doesn't bring it up. Instead, we continue as if nothing had happened, going through the remainder of the items on his list. Having an extra set of hands with me is even more useful at checkout since he helps me bag the items after the clerk scans them through. He hands her cash before I can pull out my money from my pocket.

"You didn't have to pay for that," I tell him as we carry the bags to the car. Franco opens the trunk for us with one hand, holding a gelato cone in the other.

He looks at me incredulously before replying, "Considering who I am, no one should be paying for anything when I'm around. Speaking of which," he pauses to address Franco, "where did you find that gelato?"

"Three stores down that way," Franco says, pointing in the direction of the sign. We load all the bags into the car, and Nic begins walking in that direction. Not knowing what else to do, I follow him. He slows down his pace long enough for me to catch up and mirror his stride.

"What kind of gelato do you like?" he asks me as we near the store. The smell of sweetness and comfort surrounds us as we peruse the gelato flavors listed on the menu and displayed behind a pane of glass. I don't give him an answer because the worker behind the counter is already asking what we want.

Without a second thought, I request, "Medium stracciatella in a cone." Nic considers the options in front of him, but eventually orders the same. He pays for the ice cream, and we walk back to the car at a slower pace while we lick the delicious dessert.

"That wasn't my first time in a gelato shop," he says to me, "in case you were wondering." I had been about to ask him that very thing. "Every once in a while, my mother would take my brother and me to a gelato shop in the capital city. He and I would switch up flavors each time, but I remember this one being my favorite."

"You can never go wrong with stracciatella," I agree between licks.

"You can if it's all you ever get," Franco joins in, his gelato already consumed. "You can eat those in the car, assuming you're careful not to make a mess. If I'm going to get in trouble, it's going to be for something more exciting than a few crumbs or drops of ice cream on the car interior."

Nic quips, "Such as harboring a runaway prince."

Franco chuckles and adds, "I almost wish I could take the blame for that one." Though his tone is joking, his statement is right. I'm the one who made the decision, one that nothing can make me regret. I can only hope that Director Verde understands my reasons.

WHILE NIC IS in the kitchen cooking dinner, I shower in the small bathroom connected to my bedroom. Not only does the villa have two bedrooms, but it also has two bathrooms, leaving me with one of them to myself. I take the time to wash and condition my hair, detangling my curls with my fingers and my brush. In moments like this, I'm thankful that Maria and her mother also have curly hair. Growing up, her mother would show us how to take care of it ourselves. My hair usually behaves as long as I follow her instructions and advice.

With my hair damp, I sit down next to Franco, who is patiently waiting for his favorite meal of the day. The heavenly smell spreads throughout the other rooms of our abode, and my mouth waters in eagerness. Sneaking a peek in the kitchen to see what he's making and catching him mixing ingredients will only increase my attraction to him. My mind whirls back to the elderly lady in the grocery store and her words. She hadn't told me anything I hadn't learned, but it's impossible to hold onto someone who isn't yours to begin with.

From my seat, I yell in the direction of the kitchen, "What am I smelling?"

Nic's head appears in the doorway, one of his eyebrows raised in slight surprise. Rather than answering, his head disappears back into the kitchen, only for his whole body to emerge holding the dish. "Caprese chicken," he announces as he sets it down on the trivet mat at the center of the dining room table. "Salad, plates, and utensils are in the kitchen."

"C'mon, Franco, we can't expect the prince to do everything for us," I say as I get up to help carry the other items to the dining room. Five minutes later, I'm blowing on a piece of chicken before chewing the perfectly cooked meat. Eating his cooking is a thoroughly enjoyable experience.

Nic and Franco both have suspicious expressions on their faces, and I pause my enjoyment to ask, "Why are you both looking at me like that?"

The two of them have a wordless exchange before Franco admits, "You're moaning while you eat. I'm not sure if I've ever seen someone savor their food quite so audibly before, and you know how much I love food." I feel the blush creep up my face as I become self-aware while taking my next bite.

"We didn't say you had to stop," Nic says cheekily. "I was enjoying the dinner entertainment." I roll my eyes and finish my plate without the extra sound effects. Nic unsuccessfully tries to hide his grin. I playfully shoot glares in his direction.

"Once our food is settled, we should brush up on some of your combat skills again," Franco says to Nic. "If you're going to be venturing off to another country after we reach Venezia, you could use the training. That father of yours has not been doing you any favors by keeping you isolated."

It's heartwarming to see Franco becoming friends with our tagalong. Though he will never admit it, I think he's relieved to have another guy with us on this return route. Franco and I get along well enough, but he and I aren't on the same level of friendship that I share with Dario. I might have gotten bored with just the two of us as well.

Knowing that my presence won't be necessary, I turn in for the night. Lately, I haven't been sleeping well due to the intrusion of a certain prince in my dreams. In most of them, I'm fighting another Resistance agent to protect him. The lack of sleep is catching up to me, and the two of them could use some male bonding time without me. I get ready for bed, opening the window for airflow before crawling under the sheets and blankets. Closing my eyes, I will sleep to come, but my physical exhaustion isn't enough to overcome the mental turbulence of the situation. Outside my window, I can hear Franco and Nic when they walk outside to the back patio of the villa. I'm not trying to eavesdrop, but their voices are clear as if I were out there with them.

"So, do women throw themselves at you because you're a prince, or did the whole 'being locked away in a castle' thing prevent that from happening?" Franco asks Nic. Of course, Franco would start the conversation there.

Nic laughs at the question. "When I was a teenager before my brother died, a little bit," I hear him reply. "But back then, I wasn't first in line for the throne, so most girls tended to go after my brother rather than me. Girls raised in nobility are often trained to seek the man with the highest position and power. Since he died, the ball was the first time I've attended a large social event. Leading up to the party, I felt like a deer getting ready to walk into open season."

"I guess the constant expectation to marry and all the rules regarding ladies of nobility are some of the downsides to it," Franco says thoughtfully. "There are reputations on the line. I'll bet some so-called ladies over the years have seduced men of higher rank so that an unplanned pregnancy forces him to marry her. Even common people run that risk when it comes to certain types of women."

Back in Venezia, Franco has the reputation of a heartbreaker. I am one of the few unmarried females around his age who is safe from his advances due to his respect for the mission and Director Verde. In addition, being like a younger sister to Dario means that I am also like a sister to Franco. Unfortunately for some of the other girls, they had fallen for his charms only to be dropped for the next pretty girl that came along.

"Having to think about heirs certainly complicates matters," Nic agrees. Their words become few as Franco shows him a kickboxing combination. It's minutes later when Nic returns the question, "So, does being a young agent for the Resistance mean that the women in your city throw themselves at you?"

I can picture Franco's nonchalant shrug as he answers, "A few years ago, the line of women seemed endless. The older I get, the more they want things like marriage and a family rather than passion and excitement. Plus, when you break enough hearts, word travels. Maybe once we get home, I'll be able to think about settling down. That's the whole reason I'm here on the mission instead of Dario. He found Maria, and this endeavor is too much of a gamble for someone with a fiancée waiting at home. Next combination."

Though I want to fall asleep, Franco's next question is enough to keep me conscious.

"Would you go after Lina if you were free to?" I nearly stop breathing, as if Franco had just caught me rather than Nic. Given my current location, I have no way of seeing Nic's expression or body language. I'm not sure what I'm hoping he'll divulge.

"What gave it away?" Nic asks, almost too quiet for me to pick up.

Franco says, "You pine after her the way I imagine my face looks when I'm longing for food between meals." Considering how much he eats, Franco had better not stop training if he wants to stay in shape.

"The first time I looked at her," the prince stops in the middle of his sentence, as if he's gathering his thoughts, "it was like being punched in the gut when the wind is knocked out of you. She left me breathless; she always leaves me feeling breathless. But at the same time, it's as if I'm taking that first deep breath of air after being underwater. As you can tell, I haven't figured out how to describe it. So yes, without a doubt, if things were different, I would let myself fall madly in love with her. It's taking all the willpower I have not to do so now."

"You sound like Dario when he talks about Maria," Franco says before they continue with new combinations.

Madly in love is a phrase I never thought I'd use to describe anything regarding myself because it implies not being able to think straight or make logical decisions. In different ways,

Nic and I have both been raised to use our heads instead of our hearts. "Trust your gut and be smart," had been drilled into me during scenario simulations. Until my eyes met his blue ones that fateful night not so long ago, my gut had never disagreed with my head. Logic has been working overtime to remind me that you can't fall madly in love with someone in less than a week. Infatuation is not the same as love. Infatuation is dangerous when not quashed.

I'm on the edge of drifting off to sleep when I catch Franco tell Nic, "If it turns out that your betrothed isn't alive, Lina would make a good queen. She likely doesn't see herself this way, but she's formidable. Kind and compassionate, but formidable. It may not be as hopeless as it seems." Although he meant well by his words, it wouldn't and couldn't change the outcome.

"What's on the menu tonight, Chef Niccolò?" I ask as I pull my curls back to tie them up out of my face.

He cringes at the sound of his full first name in this context. "Why not 'Chef Nic'? My full first name sounds so..."

"Royal?" I guess with a smirk. "It's a refined name for a talented chef. Now, are you going to answer my question?"

"Chicken Parmesan, a secret family recipe," he replies while pulling ingredients out of the fridge. He's sharing a secret *family* recipe. The word activated the butterflies in my stomach. He is about to share something with me that he wouldn't share with just anyone. Not that he's had many people in his life to share it with.

"When Director Verde asks why we kept you alive, we'll tell

her your cooking skills ensure that you won't outlive your usefulness," I joke as I pull an apron over my head.

He chuckles and shakes his head as he separates the ingredients. "Maybe keeping her agents well-fed will be enough to keep her from killing me herself. She might hate my father, but she was at least friendly enough to my mother. For all we know, the disappearance of the Sozzinis is exactly what united people enough to form the Resistance."

I mask my moment of realization and hold myself back from saying what I know. With the history I was taught, I should have connected that sooner. I had always assumed that the noble family backing the Resistance was living in Venezia under an alias. I had never before considered that they might be either hiding in another country or dead. The teachers always worded the account as if one of them were still alive— as if *she* were still alive.

Nic walks me through each step, showing me how to pound the meat evenly and bread each breast. He heats oil in the skillet while I finish the remaining pieces. Time moves at a faster speed as we pour the marinara on top of the fried pieces and top them with mozzarella and parsley. As dinner bakes in the oven, we clean up the mess we created during the breading process.

"You have some flour," he says and points at my face. When I'm unsuccessful at wiping it off myself, he says, "Here, let me get it."

I stand still while he raises his hand and gently brushes his fingers across my cheek to remove the white powder. My breath catches at his touch, my skin sizzling where his skin meets mine. Our eyes lock as his hand lingers on my face. This moment feels familiar, as if we've been here before. Glancing at each other's lips is instinctual, like learning how to walk or knowing when to breathe.

I pull away before his gravity becomes too strong. "I'm going to get some air," I croak. "It's a little warm in here with the oven on." The oven isn't the main source setting me on fire. I rush outside to the cool evening air, the swirls of pink and orange clouds slow dancing on the horizon. As I pace the outline of the back porch, my mind and my heart debate over whether or not I can avoid something that shows every sign of being inevitable. I've spent the better part of my life so far training how to end his, but keeping him alive is slowly killing the walls and resolve I've had around my heart. Assassins don't have space for romance.

CHAPTER 6

Niccolò

Whatever willpower I had possessed in Napoli seems to have vanished between then and tonight. One second more, and my lips would have been on hers, finally getting a taste of the tormenting object of my desires. It was masochistic of me to ask her to cook with me in the first place. After checking on the chicken baking in the oven, I glance out the small kitchen window. Her shadow glides back and forth along the same area of the back patio where Franco and I had talked about her a few nights ago. There are still two more checkpoints left of this torture—torture, both because of how easily I lose control when I'm alone with her and because I'm terrified of what my life will be like without her. I don't have to kiss her to still fall off the edge into the madness.

I tear my eyes away from the sunset—from her pacing figure —and check on dinner again. As if he has a sixth sense for knowing when food is ready, Franco pops his head through the kitchen doorway at the same time I lift the pan out of the oven. Seeing the steam rising from the chicken breasts, he gives me a nod of approval and goes to retrieve Lina from her repetitive meandering. Throughout dinner, she refuses to meet my eyes as I silently attempt to will her to look at me.

Just because we shouldn't act on our feelings doesn't mean I want her to ignore me for the remainder of this trip.

"We should play a game tonight," Franco announces, having cleared all the food from his plate. His plate is so clean, I question whether I was so distracted that I missed him licking it.

"What kind of game?" Lina asks and eyes him suspiciously.

"You know the one Director Verde encourages us to play where we either have to answer a personal question as vaguely and truthfully as possible or take a sip of alcohol. The best covers are the ones that share just enough truth, and spies frequently have to be able to toe the line in social drinking settings," Franco says with a glint in his eyes. This is a terrible idea. But with Franco around, I'm unlikely to do something I'll regret. In addition, the only alcohol we have at the villa is wine, which we are all likely to have a base tolerance for. Lina's eyes meet mine for the first time since our near kiss an hour ago. I see the woman who won't back down from any challenge or dare. We are in.

After we clear the table and wash the dishes, Lina pulls the wine out from the cupboard. I set out three wineglasses and fill them equally. "The rules are simple," Franco begins explaining. "We will each get a turn to ask another person a question, and that person has the option to either tell the truth or take a big swig of wine. Nothing is off limits. It's a favorite among the Resistance agents."

"Who gets to go first?" I ask as I distribute glasses to Lina and Franco before taking my own and sitting down.

"We'll give you the honors, since it's still technically close to your birthday," Franco replies to me.

My gaze shifts back and forth from Lina to Franco as I decide to whom to direct my first question. Franco is the one who wanted to play. "Franco, how old were you the first time you kissed a girl? Not the innocent pecks in early elementary school." Lina's expression is also curious.

He thinks for a moment before responding, "That's an easy one. Eight." Her look of shock mirrors my own.

"You were eight when you kissed a girl like *that*?" Lina asks him incredulously.

"I was an early bloomer," Franco says with a shrug. "My turn." I wait expectantly, though I know he may also choose to ask her a truth. "Nic, have you ever wished that you weren't born a prince?"

The answer is both easy and hard, but I try to clarify it anyway. "Do I resent it? No, because despite all the troubles that have come with it, I know that I'm the right person to ascend to the throne one day," I spill, hearing the words I'd said to myself spoken out loud for the first time. "But the position and responsibility come at the price of my freedom to choose. Most aspects of my life have already been chosen for me. It's ironic to be the second-most powerful man in the kingdom and be a captive to it. So no, I don't wish I weren't born a prince, but I do wish that I had more freedom to choose what that looks like."

Both my companions appear stunned by my honesty, while I feel slightly lighter having voiced those things to someone else. After a few seconds, Franco turns to Lina and gestures that it's her turn.

"Franco," she says, taking the attention off of me after my vulnerable moment in the previous round, "have you ever had a meaningful relationship?"

This one stupefies him longer than the first inquiry, but then he answers, "My mother, of course, unless you specifically meant romantic relationships." Part of me suspects he's only disclosing half the truth. After a long pause, he continues, "My first girlfriend. I thought she was the prettiest girl I had ever seen, and I felt lucky to be with her. It turned out that she had only been using me to try to get to Dario. He wasn't the least bit interested in her, though, especially after she hurt me like that." That first girl devastated him, and it shows in how he treats the girls he dates now, by how he keeps them at arm's length. The only surprise to me is that he went for the truth rather than going for the drink. Back to my turn.

"Lina, have you ever been drunk?" I ask, though I can guess the answer. With how serious the last two questions have been, I take it upon myself to lighten the mood.

"No, because I like to be in control," she says with full confidence. "No one drunk is in full control of their words and actions. That's usually when people say or do things they regret. And the whole 'liquid courage' thing is ridiculous because if you have to be under the influence of something to be brave, it's still cowardice in a way. It's usually someone afraid of embarrassment or rejection who thinks they need it to numb those negative feelings."

Franco whistles at her long-winded explanation. "That is one example of why you're Director Verde's favorite. You keep your head on straight."

I have nothing to say because I am too busy fighting my attraction to her feistiness. He had been correct when he described her as formidable. On his turn, Franco asks Lina if she's ever sneaked into the Resistance after hours. I'm not surprised that her response is "no," given that she seems to be a rule-follower except for sparing my life.

Lina takes the time to think through whom and what she'll quiz. Her eyes find mine as she asks me, "If you could bring back one person from the dead, who would it be?"

The difficulty is in selecting between my mother and my brother. To bring back my brother would be to resurrect the original heir to the throne, releasing me from my father's expectations and the duties of the crown. In that scenario, I might be free to search for my betrothed without doing so in hiding. On the other hand, it also might have meant that the Resistance would have sent someone to assassinate him instead of or in addition to me. Ultimately, the crown may have fallen back to me in the end.

Bringing back my mother held a different set of possibilities. Nothing had affected my father more than the loss of his wife and queen. The entire Kingdom might be a different place if she were alive. In addition, she would also know how to find the Sozzinis, or they would at least find a way to get a message to her. Until now, it hadn't occurred to me that they could also contact me, though that has its own risk. Choosing this is a difficult option that I'm glad I don't have to decide. I take a drink of the wine rather than dwelling on things I can't change.

"Lina, I have the same question for you," Franco says.

I observe the variety of emotions flash across her face before she also opts for the drink of wine. The memory of what she had told me that first night on the drive to Napoli flickers back to me. She doesn't know whether her parents are alive, nor would she remember enough about either of them to choose which one she would want to bring back if they are dead.

With it being my turn again, I make sure it's something I would be willing to share if someone else were to turn the question back on me. "Franco, how many children do you want?" There has to be more to him than the Lothario persona he's known for. He wouldn't have taken Dario's place on this mission if there weren't a protective side to him.

"I've always wanted a big family with lots of kids," he beams and adds, "preferably all from the same woman. I should probably work on that to make sure I don't end up with the drama from multiple baby mamas."

Lina replies with a hint of sarcasm, "Here's a thought: maybe for now on, you focus on getting to know the girls you take out on dates on a mental and emotional level. Rather than having sex with them, do something fun in a public place with plenty of lighting. It's impossible to accidentally knock someone up if you don't sleep with her. If you find someone you like, you can go on double dates with other couples, such as Dario and Maria. Your reputation isn't going to change overnight, but after going on a few dates with the same girl without seducing her, word will travel."

"Well, going on a month-long sabbatical is the perfect launching pad into my new mostly-celibate lifestyle," Franco grins. It's hard to decipher whether or not he intends to follow Lina's advice.

"Mostly?" I question when my brain catches the subtle addition to his statement. Lina struggles to keep a straight face as she looks in my direction.

"Well, you can't expect me to hold back when I do find someone I want to spend my life with," he replies with a shrug. "I'm not opposed to elopement, either." He winks, confirming the intended interpretation.

Franco goes along with the theme when he inquires, "Nic, have you ever been in love?"

Have I ever been in love? Is *love* an accurate description of the nearly all-consuming desire for Lina that permeates my every thought? I know it's not lust because at the core, it's not her body that I crave the most. I have no doubts that her physical strength, in combination with her curves, is a masterpiece, but I want her, who she is, more than that. Without the immediate likelihood of finding the daughter of Sozzini, it's become harder to remember why I keep my distance. It may not be love yet, but due to my uncertainty, I drink from the wineglass in front of me. Lina doesn't meet my eyes when I look up, and I can't read her expression. After a few moments of awkward silence, I turn to Franco expectantly. "What about you, Franco?"

"Not yet, but I'd like to think I'll find that soon," Franco says with a hopeful tone. "I've been trying to avoid that out of fear. Fear of rejection, fear of abandonment. But seeing Dario and Maria and how happy they are reminds me that when it does work out, it's worth all the risk. I don't expect love to be easy; often it's something you have to fight for, but that's what makes it worth it when you win."

An hour later, as I lie in bed, Franco's words echo through my mind. There is still no guarantee that my betrothed is alive. What if Zeta Verde tells me that she's dead, shows me proof, and is merciful enough to let me go back to my former life? At that point, I'll have to return to the castle and pretend I was in Napoli the whole time to protect Lina and Franco. Somehow, I would find a way to present the death certificate to my father and the royal cabinet to have the betrothal abolished. Then, I'd be expected to marry one of the nobles' daughters, someone titled who has been raised to rule. As much as I want to fight for Lina, I don't know how to make it work. It's frustrating when it's the one matter I wish I had a choice in, being able to choose her for longer than a couple of weeks.

THE DRIVE from Lucera to our next checkpoint in Ancona provides drastically differing views compared to the drive from Napoli to Lucera. Long stretches of the highway wind along the Adriatic coast, the green farmland to our left and the sun-glistening waters to the right. Though trees and various barriers occasionally obstruct the seascape, they help this longer drive feel shorter. The vast, seemingly never-ending nature of it beckons me and gives my mind a much-needed reprieve. Whether conscious or not, Lina has been avoiding me since we ended the game last night. Franco turns on the radio a half hour into the drive when neither of us will talk to fill the space.

I'm disappointed when the highway veers inland again, replacing the sea with buildings or trees. Still, this whole experience of seeing my country through the eyes of ordinary people is enough to make everything worthwhile. I glance at the map Franco had handed me when we got in the car. My fingers trace the curves of the highway, my eyes noting the way it skates in and out from the sea like two lovers in an intricate dance. Another stretch along the sea lies ahead, where the highway cuts through several coastal cities.

The population of Ancona is three times that of Lucera. As Franco had informed me during breakfast this morning, it is not known for beaches even though it's a coastal town. Sitting at the top of rocky cliffs by the sea, the city has several spots offering panoramic views. There may be a beach or two that can be hiked to from the cliffs, but the majority of the seafront consists of ports and marinas for boats and shipping. "It's not like the beaches in Venezia," he had concluded. It's uncertain whether I'll be welcome to stay for long in Venezia, or if doing so would be wise. If I have the option to, I'll be happy to see the beaches Lina and Franco are native to.

As our next destination grows nearer, I know Lina must be stir crazy because I'm feeling restless myself. Due to the drive being slightly longer, we had left earlier to reach Ancona by lunch, which means that the more my stomach rumbles, the closer we must be. I know by the frequency and density of buildings that we are nearing the restaurant chosen by the Resistance contacts in this city.

Ristorante L'Ascensore isn't the hole-in-the-wall restaurant I had anticipated in a port town, but rather an upscale, built-into-the-cliff dining experience that provides panoramic views of the sea. The structure was built and still functions as a lift. The owner opened a restaurant in the Passetto, the local name for the elevator. When Franco gives the hostess his name, she leads us onto the terrace where our hosts are basking in the midday sunlight and sea breeze. Whatever exhaustion I'd felt seems to melt away in the relaxing ambiance. Rather than a married couple, our hosts are a man and his younger sister, the latter of whom appears close to our age.

The brother, Rafael, eyes me as if he's trying to place how he knows me. I know I've never met him before, but it doesn't mean that certain Resistance agents can't procure an image of me. If he's suspicious of my presence with the other two, he doesn't let on beyond that. My training growing up included extensive sessions on keeping my composure under any circumstance. Rafael's sister Chiara is quieter and more subdued compared to her older brother, who carries the conversation. I also choose to dwell in the shadows as much as I can to focus on observing my surroundings.

Rafael has a gold band on his left hand, meaning he's likely married. Chiara's hand does not have a ring on it. Given the way she's stealing glances to look at Franco, it may be safe to assume that she doesn't have a boyfriend either. Or she does, but it's not serious enough for her to ignore her obvious attraction to my friend. Her presence confirms that she is part of the Resistance too, and since she doesn't live in Venezia, she's unlikely to be aware of his reputation. I watch the way Franco and Chiara look at each other when they think no one else is paying attention. Is that what he's noticed between me and Lina? Are we this conspicuous?

Lina interjects in Rafael's ramblings about his family's business in the city with questions about shipping routes and connections to other countries nearby. Even here, she doesn't look me in the eye. I know she also notices the silent exchange with Franco and Chiara. Maybe it's her way to communicate that she needs space, but she can tell me that without giving me the cold shoulder. Rafael pays the check without looking at the bill, the way someone accustomed to wealth does—the way I would.

Rather than handing us the keys and address, Rafael hands them to his sister and tells us, "Chiara will show you to the villa and make sure you're settled for the week." Clearly, either he hasn't noticed the way Franco is eyeing his little sister, or he trusts mine and Lina's presence will provide enough supervision. Lina graciously offers the front passenger seat to Chiara and joins me in the backseat, all without looking me in the eye again. I distract myself from Lina's uninviting presence by eavesdropping on Franco and Chiara during the short drive.

Chiara's family's money is evident in the villa where Franco parks the car. She shows us all six bedrooms and bathrooms, the fully stocked fridge, and the pool with private access. "If you want a good beach to visit, you can drive south to Portonovo Beach," she informs us when Franco asks about the local beaches for my sake. "It gets crowded on the weekends, but during the week is usually the best time."

"And, what's the best time if I want to see you?" Franco flirts with her. Her blush is my cue to retrieve the suitcases from the car. Without a glance in my direction, he tosses the keys to me.

I carry Lina's suitcase to the door of the suite she disappeared into, knock, and then proceed with the remainder of the luggage. Lina is so quiet when she opens the door and walks out that I jump when I find her next to me. She puts her finger to her lips to shush me before we tiptoe through the main living area, past the flirting couple, and out the front door.

"I thought you could use some help since Franco is preoccupied," she says as she grabs one of the two remaining bags. "Plus, neither of you would let me help the last two times."

"Do you think we need to rescue his new preoccupation?" I ask her quietly as we walk back toward the house. Franco and Chiara are still talking, but the space between their bodies has diminished somewhat.

Lina waits until we're out of earshot to respond. "I'm not sure, but I would rather not find out that these walls aren't soundproof." We both shudder at the thought of hearing that at night. Right now, it's as if she's flipped a switch and is back to her usual self.

After our hands are empty of the luggage, I gently grab her arm to stop her from walking away. "Lina, are we okay?" To her credit, she looks at me this time.

"Yeah, I think that wine got to me a little last night," she lies. If I hadn't been carefully studying her facial expressions over the past ten days, I would have bought it. Despite my desire to call her out on it and insist on the truth, I release her arm and let her go back to her room.

"You and your friends should come out to the club tonight," Chiara says to Franco when I walk past them to the kitchen. "I have the perfect dress that I could lend to Lina."

I pause then backtrack, making it clear that I had heard that part of the conversation. "Did you say club? How far is it from here?" I ask her excitedly.

"A CLUB?" Lina gapes at us incredulously from across the dinner table. "What makes you think going to a club is a good idea?"

Franco reassures her, "No one recognizes Nic, and you two have been weird around each other all day. We could all use a little fun outside the villa walls. You have to come and make sure Nic and I don't do anything stupid. Plus, I promised Chiara I would go. It is a public place, like you had suggested."

She turns to me, expecting me to side with her on this, but I merely shrug. "Tonight may be my only opportunity to go to a club," I admit to her.

An hour later, Franco is driving the car while I'm in the passenger seat, giving directions. Lina had changed into a dress and heels that, if I had any right to an opinion, I wouldn't want her to wear to a place like this. She's the one most likely to attract attention tonight. Franco parks the car a few blocks away and hands the keys to Lina as we walk toward Club Del Mare.

"Since you don't like to get drunk, you're the designated driver," he says, and she doesn't object. She slips the key into a secret compartment on the side of her stiletto boots. When we turn the last corner, it's abundantly clear that Chiara has invited us to one of the most popular nightclubs in the city. Lines of people wait at the entrance for their turn. As we pass the front door, Chiara appears and yells Franco's name, gesturing for us to join her inside. The security guard lets us through without a second glance as if we were special guests.

The volume of the music and the people is so loud that I can barely hear myself think. Chiara's hand is holding Franco's as we push past people to the VIP area. Not wanting to hang out in the crowd most likely to recognize a prince, I find a seat at the bar and order a Negroni. I shift my body at an angle that allows me to keep an eye on my friends as I sip the drink the bartender hands me. I pull out a large bill and slide it to him with the instructions, "If I start to get low, give me a refill." Three drinks later, my head finally feels some of the effects of the alcohol. Lina may have strong opinions regarding the use of liquid courage, but approaching her isn't something easily done sober.

She watches me as I stalk toward her position at the edge of the VIP group. With a raised eyebrow, she asks me, "Done already?"

Unsure of whether she's asking if I'm done drinking or done being here, I state my purpose as a question: "Will you dance with me?" Hand stretched out toward her, I feel a sense of déjà vu. This time, of course, is less formal in every sense. This time, I can't coerce her into it by using my birthday or my title. She's learned she can say no to me without consequence other than my disappointment. In a mere ten days, she's discovered that when she pushes me away, I'll keep coming back. At least, until we reach Venezia.

Just like she had before, she accepts my invitation. Hand in hand, we walk to the makeshift dance floor and mimic the movements of the other couples around us. This type of dancing is vastly different from the waltz we danced on my birthday, her body moving closer to mine in time with the pulsing rhythm. I fight to ignore the way she smells like coconut or the way her dress accentuates her curves. My eyes remain on her face as she enjoys this carefree moment. After a few songs, she says in my ear, "I need to use the restroom. I'll be right back."

While I wait for her return, I chug a much-needed glass of water at the bar. Two songs later, I also decide to use the restroom, hoping to run into her on my way. I don't see her in the line on the women's side, so I proceed to use the men's before venturing back out to search for her. When I walk back into the hallway after using the restroom, my ears pick up the sound of her voice. I head in the general direction until I spot her cornered by a stranger whose back is turned to me.

"I said, 'I'm not interested,'" she warns him in a tone that would ward off any gentleman. This guy doesn't seem to get the message, though. He leans in closer, and I know this won't be pretty. Lina is perfectly capable of protecting herself, of this I'm certain, but Franco was sent on the mission with her for a reason. In another part of the room, Franco woos a future wife or a casual fling, depending on their preference.

I place my hand on the man's shoulder and reiterate, "She said she's not interested." His whole body turns toward me, the annoyance evident on his face. Lina's face, which had been calm seconds before, now holds a hint of fear. Not fear for herself; fear for me. I straighten my spine, readying myself for what comes next. I react to his moving fist fast enough to dodge the brunt of his punch, but something scratches the skin across my right cheek. Within seconds, the security guard intervenes, physically removing the man from the club. Blood trickles from the stinging cut.

Lina hurries to the bartender and comes back carrying a few napkins in her hand. "Here, hold that against your cheek to try to stop the bleeding," she demands. "I'm going to tell Franco that we're going back to the villa. I need to get that cut of yours cleaned up." Adept at slipping through crowds, she's back in less than a minute without Franco.

"Chiara is giving him a ride?" I guess, and she nods and heads toward the exit. She confirms that the man who hit me has already left before gesturing for me to follow her. Walking while holding a napkin to part of my face proves to be frustrating, but anytime I drop my hand, she shoots me a glare. Without a mirror, I have no way to know if her concern is warranted.

When we get in the car, she drives at a speed faster than she was willing to go in my Maserati. "You didn't have to do that," she says quietly, her dark eyes fixed on the road. "I saw that he was wearing a family ring on his hand. Something like that can cause damage to a tooth or an eye. I think that's what cut your face." I hadn't noticed the ring, but I also hadn't thought to. I'm used to noble men having signet rings; until tonight, I didn't know of common families having them as well.

"Just because you can take down a guy that size on your own doesn't mean you should have to," I argue with her. "What kind of man would I be if I stood and watched rather than try to protect you? I'm the future king, and I don't take that lightly. True kings are supposed to be honorable and willing to step in on behalf of the innocent."

Lina remains quiet and focused on the road, waiting until the car is parked at the entrance of the villa to continue our conversation. She redirects her focus to me and softly says, "I said that you didn't have to, not that you shouldn't have or that I didn't want you to. Thank you for putting your pretty face at risk for me. Let's go inside and get that cleaned up."

As soon as we're inside, she kicks off her stilettos, the only indication she's shown of the heels' discomfort. "My cut can wait another five minutes if you want to change," I tell her, knowing that she wants to get out of the short dress (I'll have to thank Chiara for that) almost as much as the shoes she's already removed. She smiles gratefully and hurries to her room. I go to my bedroom to do the same, being careful not to let my wounded cheek touch my shirt or pajamas. There's a soft knock at my door, preceded by Lina entering in her silk pajamas with a first aid kit in her hand.

"Sit," she demands, pointing to the edge of the bed. Without argument, I do what she says and watch as she rifles through the box for supplies. She sets the box on the floor and sits next to me. "First, I need to clean and disinfect the cut since we have no idea where that ring has been. Then, if the bleeding has slowed, I'll put a bandage on it."

"Lina, I know how this works," I say and give her a small smile.

Unamused, she pours the saline onto the cloth and warns, "This might sting a little." She places her right hand under my jaw to steady my head and uses her left to clean my right cheek. I'm distracted by the concentration on her face as she leans close, and I savor the electricity I feel where her skin touches mine. I count the faint freckles on her cheeks that I had noticed when dancing with her at the ball. Without makeup, she's still breathtakingly beautiful. "The good news is that you won't need stitches. The bleeding seems to have slowed down. Hopefully, it doesn't leave much of a scar."

"Here I was hoping to have a scar as proof that I saved you once," I joke, warranting an eye-roll from her. My face feels cold when her hands leave to get the bandage. Carefully and slowly, she smooths the bandage over the wound, her face only a few inches from mine.

Whether it's from the leftover alcohol in my system or the natural effect she has on me, I decide that if she doesn't pull away and leave, I'm going for it this time. My life choices are limited, but I can choose her for the next two weeks, even if it's not as long-term as I want.

I hesitantly close the distance between our lips, mine meeting hers in a whisper of a kiss, gentle and tender. It's the type of innocent first kiss a prince should give to his sweetheart. I pull back just far enough to read her eyes, to let her decide the next step. My heart nearly stops at the softness and vulnerability I can see in her dark irises. Her hands find their way to the back of my head and into my hair, forcing my lips back down to hers.

Lina's kiss is more demanding, more consuming, more everything. I taste the sweetness of the virgin cocktail she had been drinking at the club. Our hearts race and breaths mingle as the kiss deepens. Without thinking and without breaking contact, we lie across the bed, my hands on her waist as her fingers intertwine and tangle with my hair. Her body moves flush against mine, and the heat only adds to the fire coursing through my veins. Through the haze of desire, alarm bells ring in my head, reminding me not to go too far.

"Lina," I croak out when her lips trail away from mine to trace my jawline. My blood rushes as her mouth moves to my neck. I try again, "Lina," this time, gently grabbing her wrists with my hands. Her dazed eyes meet mine, her chest rising and falling with labored breath. I wait for the breathing to slow, for her eyes to focus, and enough blood to return to my brain. When I'm certain she's thinking clearly again, I let go of her wrists. "We can't do that—I have to think about the future. I can't risk a possible illegitimate child, especially not as the eldest."

"And that wouldn't be fair to her," Lina adds, the bittersweetness of her tone cutting through me.

"It wouldn't be fair to anyone," I continue. "Even if I knew right now that my betrothal was void, I still wouldn't cross that line without exchanging vows first. I'm just the handsome prince who's falling for you, but I can't promise you forever. I wish I could be the man to give you everything you want."

She nods in agreement and then asks, "As much as I've tried to ignore it, it's pretty obvious how you feel about me. Why kiss me now after days of perfect control?"

It is a fair question, considering I had been the one who pulled away from her in the beginning. "Because I realized that for the rest of my life, any significant choice I have will be based on duty or law. I only have two more weeks where I can be free enough to decide something without that, and I want to spend that small amount of time kissing you and hoping that's enough to show you how I feel. Just kissing."

"You're talking to a Resistance agent here," she jokes as she stands up. "I know how boundaries work. No more bedrooms. Now that your face is patched up, I'm going to my separate bedroom and bathroom. Goodnight."

I should feel guilty for crossing that line with Lina, but I'm still smiling when I manage to fall asleep.

CHAPTER 7

Adelina

Hot water soothes my tense muscles as my mind flashes back to last night, to the way he kissed me. Being in his arms felt like…it felt like coming home in a way. It's as if he instinctively knew how to kiss me. He was the one who had been drinking last night, yet I was the one who was so drunk that I might have let things escalate if he hadn't stopped me.

"It's impossible to accidentally knock someone up if you don't sleep with her," were the words I had told Franco a few nights ago. Somehow, I had almost put myself in that position. What a mess that would have been, having to explain that to Director Verde. It's one thing to help the prince I was supposed to kill escape his father's control; it's another to be pregnant with his child after only knowing him for ten days. Fortunately, nothing happened because he's a gentleman. I need to be better about sticking to my boundaries.

Nic was still asleep when I woke up this morning, and there was no trace or indication that Franco had even come home. If he doesn't turn up by lunch, Nic and I will have to search for him.

Once I'm dressed, I venture into the kitchen to find Nic making breakfast and a cappuccino already waiting for me. "Did Franco not come back last night?" he asks me, turning his head to look at me. Are his eyes always that blue, like the depths of the Adriatic?

"I don't think so," I reply. "I was a bit preoccupied, though. From what I can tell, he didn't sleep in his room."

Nic smirks when I mention being preoccupied, unleashing butterflies in my stomach. He steps toward me and takes my cup of coffee from my hands to set it down on the counter. Then, with his hands caressing either side of my face, he kisses me slowly and softly. "Good morning, beautiful Adelina," he whispers with his eyes closed and forehead resting against mine. There is something intimate about the way he uses my full first name rather than the usual nickname.

"Good morning, Niccolò." I smile as he steps away to check on the food.

"It would seem we are on a full first-name basis now," he points out while scooping two servings of the frittata onto plates for us. He carries the plates to the dining room table, and I follow him with both our cups of coffee. I watch him as we eat, taking in his still-unruly hair and bandaged cheek. I'll need to check on his cut today to see how it's healing. A five o'clock shadow reveals that he hasn't shaved yet today. Did he come straight to the kitchen after waking up?

He's also watching me, though trying to be less obvious about it. As my mind reflects on last night's events, I conclude that I may not find someone else who can give me everything I want. What I want is sitting in front of me, looking at me with complete adoration. What I want is a lifetime with him, but I'll take whatever time I can get. If I feel myself getting carried away with the fantasy, I remind myself that he's practically engaged. I have to remember her, his father, and our lives beyond these two weeks to keep myself from being reckless. Snapping back to the present moment, I carry the empty dishes to the kitchen. His arms wrap around my waist from behind as he rests his head on top of mine.

"You shouldn't feel guilty," he tells me as his scent envelopes me. "I'm the one who kissed you, and I'm the one responsible for what I do or don't do. Even though I'm betrothed, I'm not the one who made any vows or commitments to her. The only promises I've made are the ones to myself. When I become king, I will change the law that allows parents to bind their kids to this type of betrothal. As much as I want to honor my mother's wishes, I don't think this situation is what she would have wanted for me."

Two weeks is a short time compared to decades. Apprehension is a better way to describe my emotional state because now, going home to the one place I thought I would look forward to returning to, will mean saying goodbye to him. He doesn't let go of my waist when I've put away the dishes, so I turn around to face him. I resist the immediate urge to kiss him again. "Just like I hope Director Verde will realize why I didn't follow through on her instructions to kill you when she sees your character," I admit to him.

His eyes light up before he kisses me. I drown in the feel of his smile against my lips, his hands gripping my waist. We lose sense of our surroundings until we hear the front door close. Franco walks in faster than Nic and I can pull apart. My safety detail looks at both of us with a knowing expression. "Don't stop on my account. I'd rather you two be all over each other than the awkward cold shoulder stuff yesterday. As long as you're not loud at night or pregnant before we reach Venezia, do what you want. I'm not kidding about the baby part. Director Verde will have my head, too, for not keeping you from doing something stupid."

My face flushes red as Nic chuckles with a shake of his head. "No illegitimate children will be had here," the prince promises. "Lina is too good to be subject to the life of a mistress." I'm both relieved that he sees me as more than that, while also saddened by the fact that being a mistress would be the only way to be with him once he finds his betrothed. Of course, I wouldn't let myself be in that situation, nor is he the type to break his marriage vows by having a mistress. We are at a stalemate at the end of this trip.

"You're right about that," Franco agrees, and I remember the overheard conversation where he told Nic I could be a queen.

Nic turns the conversation's focus to Franco. "What about you? Neither of us heard you come home last night. Do we need to be concerned about Chiara?"

Franco blushes, a reaction I've never seen on him. He sheepishly answers, "I kissed her, that's all. And I probably touched her less than you two have touched each other in the past twelve hours. I drank too much, and she was tired, so I slept on her couch. She dropped me off here after we had breakfast together. I will be spending more time with her while we're in Ancona."

Nic walks over to Franco and pats him on the back. "Think she could be someone you would want to settle down with?" It's peculiar how, in this instance, Franco's level of interest can be gauged by whether he sees a future with Chiara or not. Meanwhile, Nic had essentially told me that he loves me—or likely will soon—knowing full well that we have no future. How can he possibly know that so definitively to be able to say it?

"I think there's a possibility," Franco says uncertainly. He has the look of a man willing to move to be with the woman he loves, even though it's an infatuation. Months from now, Dario and Maria will be married, Franco will likely be moving to Ancona if things with Chiara go well while we're

here, Nic and the Sozzini daughter will be married, and I...
still have no idea what my future looks like. Given how
drastically different the last ten days have been from what I
had planned or imagined, I speculate that not knowing what
the future holds isn't particularly daunting. Any day could
bring an event that changes my path for years to come. Before
yesterday, Franco hadn't yet visited Ancona nor met Chiara.
The future is always subject to change.

Franco dismisses himself to take a much-needed shower
before Chiara comes by to take all of us sightseeing. I firmly
suggest to Nic that he do the same with the agreement that I'll
check on his wound when he's clean and dressed. He sweetly
kisses my forehead on his way to follow my instructions. I lie
across the couch in the living room and close my eyes to
collect my thoughts better.

Love holds the connotation of something lasting, something
that shouldn't fade away after two weeks. But just because
we'll be separated at the end of these two weeks doesn't
mean his love for me will stop the moment he leaves. The
real, true, infinitesimal love that exists in Maria's novels
endures long after the couple has been separated. Time and
distance will change the intensity of it undoubtedly, but what
if years from now, there's enough of it preserved in our hearts
that we still think of each other and treasure the fortnight
with the days that led up to it. What if I find myself telling
my future daughter the story of how I fell in love with a
prince once? Maybe what makes this love is simply that I'm
putting him above my needs and desires by letting him go in
the end.

Franco is the first to emerge from the hallway that leads to the
bedrooms. "I'm assuming you didn't do the deed," he says as
he sits on the other couch a few feet away.

"He's as honorable as they come," I confirm. "No clothes
were removed, and hands stayed in safe zones."

"He's good for you, even if all you glean from this is how to let someone in," he says with surprising insight. "But I have a good feeling about it, which I know isn't anything concrete or rational at all." I roll my eyes, but I appreciate the kind gesture anyway. It is nice knowing that our one friend who has watched the progression believes that this could end in anything other than two broken hearts.

Nic joins us, taking the seat next to Franco. The young prince's dark hair is damp, and the bandage has been removed. I get up to inspect it closer. A few hours have helped it scab over, but it still looks delicate. To ease my concerns, I retrieve a fresh bandage from the first aid kit in my room and apply it over the scab as precisely as I had last night, right before that first kiss.

Franco interrupts my thoughts by saying, "Actually, I take it back. Please don't make out in front of me. Now I see how this," he points back and forth from Nic to me, "happened last night." I make a mental note about how perceptive Franco is. Dario had mentioned that fact about Franco to me before, but his friend likes to give the impression of ignorance. Good agents aren't ignorant, though.

Chiara knocks at the villa's front door to signal the start of our day plans. Franco drives as Chiara gives him directions from the front passenger seat, leaving Nic and me in the backseat holding hands. The stroke of his thumb across my skin sends shivers through my body. In my peripheral vision, I see his smug smile at the knowledge of how his touch affects me.

At Chiara's leading, we park on what appears to be a random street. As we walk toward the cloaked pathway, Franco's hand rests on the small of her back, a gesture of both intimacy and protection. From my recollection, he's never done that with any of his "conquests" in Venezia. I want to ask them how they can feel so comfortable with each other after only a day, but one glance toward Nic's figure walking in sync with mine renders the question needless. The first full day in Napoli had only been the day after I met the prince at his ball, and there had been a near assassination attempt that should have caused a great distance between us. Instead, his obscure betrothal had been the only thing keeping his lips from mine a mere twenty-four hours after I had spared him. I'm still undecided which of us is the most masochistic in all this.

"This is the Grotta Azzurra Pathway," Chiara informs as we follow her down the path of steps leading to the shore. The sound of sea waves fills my eardrums as we descend the trail. The blue of the sky and the blue of the water are familiar shades, equally as breathtaking as they are in Nic's eyes. I slow down for a moment to fully embrace the beauty of the panoramic scene from this height. Nic reflects my movement, his eyes searching my face. His irises are a lighter blue in the sunlight compared to the deeper electric color they were last night.

"This is a spectacular view," he says, the statement cheesy with his gaze more on me than the sea below. I must be cheesy as well because his presence adds to the panoramic seascape. Noting that Franco and Chiara are far enough ahead to provide us some privacy, I pull him in for what I intend to be a short kiss. He has other ideas, though, groaning when my lips leave his. With our fingers intertwined, I drag him along to catch up with our friends. I feel the moment he relents and starts walking again.

The rocky shoreline at the bottom isn't what attracts tourists to these spots, but rather the caves built into the side of the cliff. With a twinge of homesickness, I think about Maria and how much she would love to see the way the green vegetation thrives on the cliffs despite the rocky terrain. I wonder whether she would be glad at how much the prince makes me happy or sad at how complicated it is. How would she react to watching our city's worst womanizer stare at

Chiara in unfiltered adoration, identical to the way Dario looks at her?

"I think we've been a good influence on him," I say to Nic as we observe how careful Franco is not to take things too far too quickly. "Maybe it's too soon to say, but that's not the same guy who left Venezia with me."

"Do you think he'll be a bit depressed when we have to leave?" Nic asks with concern in his voice.

"Depends on how they leave things," I guess. "Either they'll end whatever relationship they have going, or he'll promise to return and make things work. The latter may be less depressing since it holds the possibility of a future." Though I hadn't meant to, some of my sadness crept in with my words.

He picks up on it as well, gently placing both his hands on either side of my face to force me to look at him. "Adelina, if I were anyone else in any other position, I would be making those types of promises to you. You know that, but my hands are tied by people and bloodlines that are outside my control or ability to change. While there is still a possibility that I won't find my betrothed alive, I'm still the crown prince. A future with me would still come at a high price: a position with duties and responsibilities. You would have to leave everyone and everything you've ever known, not to mention dealing with my father."

"Your father, whom we all suspect is the reason you're having to track down your betrothed," I point out to him.

"I'll figure that out when the time comes," he says in an exhausted voice. There is nothing to figure out. He would have to do the one thing guaranteed to keep her safe, and the thought makes me jealous. Assuming marriage is enough to keep her safe. "I can't live in a world of hypotheticals when there are so many unknowns. We won't have any answers until we face Director Verde. In this moment, I want to spend every second I can with you. I'm going to need you to get out of your head and stop thinking ahead so that we can enjoy our time together." He embraces me in a hug, his strong arms wrapped around me. Before he lets go, he kisses the top of my head.

The shipyards are what make Ancona special. When tourism was one of the largest industries in Lazio, cruise ships and ferries would frequently depart from its ports. Even without that, dozens of ferries disembark from Ancona daily. For centuries, Ancona has been a key port for commercial trade and naval ships. Not only would this be an ideal location for the Resistance to expand and build a base, but it would also be an ideal place to come if one wanted to stow away on a ship to another country. If Nic's betrothed is in another country and the Resistance supports him, he may have to leave on one of these ships undercover.

"I'm not a big fan of baseball caps," the prince quietly complains to me as we walk a few steps behind Franco and Chiara toward Lanterna Rossa. The red lighthouse doesn't seem as tall as I would have imagined, but its color is enough of a contrast in comparison to the ocean blue surrounding it.

Ensuring Chiara doesn't hear something she shouldn't, I lean in and whisper, "You're the one who insisted on coming with us today. Any one of those yachts could have a noble on board who would recognize you without a disguise. I shouldn't have even let you come with us to the club."

"Let me?" He doesn't try to hide the irritation in his tone. "Assassination orders aside, you don't have the authority to let me do anything. Even if I weren't a prince, I am still a grown man who is capable of making his own decisions about his safety."

"You're a prince who has spent the last decade or so of his life either at the castle or his mother's family home," I say with a desperation I wish I didn't feel. "Look, this isn't just about you. I was also at that ball with you, and some guests saw us dancing together. While I have doubts that any of them would recognize me here, they would be able to place where they saw me if they recognized you. That would put us both in danger."

Before he can respond, we've arrived at the iconic red lighthouse that juts out into the water near the ship routes.

"This is a popular place for couples to come on evening strolls," Chiara tells us as we bask in the sunshine and ocean breeze. Something about Ancona reminds me of home in a way that makes me eager to see the streets of Venezia again.

Apart from when Chiara stops to give us facts about her city, she and Franco seem to be lost in their own world for the majority of our walking tour. To conclude our day's excursion, Chiara takes us to a fountain called Fontana del Calamo.

"Is this the fountain you mentioned yesterday?" Franco asks as he cups his hands to collect enough water from the spout for a drink. With the amount of walking we've been doing, we could all use hydration.

Chiara smiles at his question. "Yes, this is the one. The tradition is that if you take a drink from this fountain, you'll return to Ancona." Franco makes a show of taking a drink of water from each of the thirteen spouts along the fountain before winking at her. Tradition or not, the water is inviting to my parched throat. Niccolò, on the other hand, might need tradition on his side if he's to return.

When we get back to the villa, Franco kisses Chiara goodbye like a scene out of a movie. The wind blows her hair at the exact angle to be flattering rather than in their face. I would feel self-conscious about watching their interaction if it weren't so picture-perfect. Nic waits for me at the door and holds it open for me. Rather than walking past him, I wrap my arms around him in a hug. He reciprocates and rests his chin on my head. I breathe in the scent of his pine soap mingled with the sea breeze. His embrace is everything warm and safe as it cocoons me. I almost prefer this feeling of comfort over the blazing fire and electricity of his lips.

"I'm going back out to look for a gift for Chiara if either of you wants to come," Franco says to us.

"I was thinking about going for a swim," I reply, looking up at Nic for his decision.

He scrutinizes me, likely remembering what just happened last night, and says, "I'm going to accompany Franco. There are a few things I want to pick up at the supermarket for a recipe I want to make for dinner tonight." He releases me and walks back out the door with Franco, leaving me with some alone time. Unfortunately, I won't be able to eavesdrop on their conversation about me that they'll undoubtedly be having. With how transparent Nic has been recently, I'm certain he won't say anything that he isn't willing to tell me later.

CHAPTER 8

Niccolò

L
ina seems relieved to have the pool to herself as I join
Franco in the car. As tempting as it is to stay behind,
it's the temptation that convinces me to take the
opportunity to get some time away from her. The last thing I
need is to be alone with her while she's wearing a swimsuit.

"I'm surprised you chose me over her, but I'm flattered
regardless," Franco says as he puts on his seatbelt.

"I don't trust myself alone with her at the moment," I admit
with gritted teeth.

Franco laughs at my plight, but then his face expresses
sympathy. "If pregnancy and an illegitimate child are what
you're trying to avoid, you can buy condoms. They're not
guaranteed to prevent it, but it's a high enough effectiveness.
Assuming one doesn't break, you would be safe."

"That's not the only reason why," I explain to him. "It
wouldn't be just sex with us. I don't think it's ever 'just sex,'
though you may disagree with my perspective. It's the most
intimate part of yourself that you can share with another
person. With Lina, I would be giving her my entire being in

the process, only to have to leave her to find another woman. And then that woman whose family's flight from the country was caused by my father's words and actions will marry a man who made love to someone else while knowing she and the betrothal existed. Condoms might prevent pregnancy, but they can't prevent that mess of a consequence. Life is much easier when you choose to wait until marriage."

I expect Franco to laugh again or to contradict something I said, but he's contemplative. "You're undoubtedly a virgin, but I mean that as a compliment," he says carefully. "Sometimes, I wish I could reverse time and be that way again. Eventually, Chiara is going to find out how long my list is, and I can only pray that it doesn't scare her away. When you find your betrothed, you'll be able to tell her that even though you had strong feelings for someone else, you went against your desires because you treasure the marital bed or something sappy like that. She'll fall for it, as girls do."

"Well, I hope she finds my lack of experience reassuring since it'll mean I'll never compare sleeping with her to a past lover," I add. "She won't ever have to think, 'Did he do this with her?'"

Franco's smile is small, but he says, "You're a good guy. Selfless, too, for the most part. Whomever Lina ends up with will also be grateful that you didn't take her virtue. Imagine trying to pursue a girl who had previously slept with a charming prince."

"I think that's why so many nobles in the past had mistresses," I surmise with a shake of my head. "The only social and political position higher than the crown prince is king, and I would highly advise against any woman getting involved with my father. My mother's death still haunts him. For all his faults, I know he was faithful to her while she was alive."

"That does make sense why women would subject themselves to that," he admits. "Apart from the money and comfort, knowing the king is willingly in your bed is an unacknowledged position of power, albeit a dangerous place if you refuse him. But poor men have had mistresses too, who were well aware of their position. If the chemistry is explosive, one might be willing to do anything to keep that, even if it means having or being a side piece. Life is much simpler if you can marry someone you have that connection with." Franco offers me a wry smile.

"Ah, well, my life has never been that simple."

"When you said you wanted to buy her a gift, I didn't think you meant jewelry," I say to Franco, who is browsing the bracelet selection. Most of them are simple and inexpensive, made from metals like gold and silver without the addition of pricy diamonds or precious stones. The sparkle of a ruby catches my eye, like the red of the dress Lina was wearing on the night we met. Gifting her jewelry may be crossing a line and taking a risk that she'll even accept the gesture, but the gold set pendant is the type of necklace I can picture her wearing.

Franco catches me as I deliberate over the pros and cons. "She'll love the necklace, but she'll hate that you bought her jewelry because it'll be another physical item to remind her of you when you're gone," Franco says in one of his deeply insightful moments. "It's a toss-up whether she'll throw it into the Venetian Lagoon or keep it long enough for the painful parts to fade." While I hope for the latter, the former is what I visualize. I choose to hope despite my misgivings, and I purchase the pendant anyway.

"Is there a special reason why you bought a bracelet for Chiara, or is it meant to be a physical reminder of you?" I ask Franco when we're on the way to the supermarket.

"I plan on asking her to be my girlfriend," he discloses. "It's not often that I make it to the third date with a girl, and I want to be able to spend some of my time here this trip being able to call her that."

"You're telling me that the infamous womanizer Franco is committing to one girl?" I feign shock, having seen this as a possibility.

He shrugs off my reaction. "This Franco has been subject to watching an agent trained to be an assassin spare her target, only to fall for him, and her affections for him are not unrequited. Anything is possible as far as I'm concerned." I want to believe him, that anything is possible.

I pick up a few ingredients from the store while Franco waits in the car. Thanks to Lina's instructions and the previous supermarket trips, it's an easy endeavor to do by myself. I'm going to miss the little freedoms like being able to pick out my produce from the store and going on impromptu gelato trips. By the time we return to the house, Lina is sitting in the living room reading a book, her damp hair gathered over her left shoulder. She's engrossed in whatever novel she's holding. I lean down and kiss her bare right shoulder before sneaking a peek at what has her attention.

"It's one of Maria's books," she tells me without looking up. Seeing that she's near the end of a chapter, I wait for her to finish. "*Jane Eyre*."

"Ah, that one," I say, having read it during a rainy day in the castle library. "Are you an avid reader?"

Franco walks past and answers my question, "She was always holding a book on her day off. Whether she's reading all those novels is a mystery to most of us."

Lina blushes and confesses, "I had the habit of using Maria's novels to hide the maps and blueprints I needed to memorize."

"Maps and blueprints of what?" I question, even though I remember what Franco had told me about her studying.

She admits bashfully, "The castle, the various routes to and from your chamber."

"Wow, obsessed with me before we had even met. I have to say, I'm flattered," I tease her. "But really, you're thorough and a good student. I admire your discipline and hard work, even if it was meant at my expense." She ruffles my hair playfully, and I pretend to glare at her.

"I've also memorized all the streets and alleys of both Venezia and the capital city, so it wasn't personal," she says shyly. She's cavalier whenever I bring up her skills and talents as if she doesn't see herself for how incredible she is. Maybe it's humility on her end because she's not insecure about it. Someone like her really would make a good queen.

Franco interrupts our conversation by showing Lina the bracelet he purchased for Chiara. "I plan on asking her to be my girlfriend over dinner tomorrow night," he tells her. "Which also means that you two will have the villa to yourselves for a few hours. I trust that you both will utilize good sense and not put each other in a compromising position."

We both look at Franco quizzically. Lina is the first to respond. "Franco, how many times do we have to tell you that we're not going to let that happen? As much as we both might want to, we understand that it's not what's best for each other. Nic and I will be fine on our own for a few hours."

"Oh, I trust you both implicitly," he says. "It's just fun being able to embarrass you for once. I always wondered what Lina would be like when she's in love, and it's amusing to watch."

In love are the words he uses to describe her feelings for me, and she doesn't deny the validity of his statement. It's how I've labeled my feelings for her in my head, and it may have slipped out a few times. I had told her that I kissed her because I wanted her to remember me as the prince who was falling for her, but that doesn't count as an official declaration of love. Franco may have just given me the perfect opportunity for such a gesture.

"This is the dome you wanted to see up close, is it not?" Chiara asks as our uphill walk leads us to the Cattedrale di San Ciriaco.

To our left is a stunning view of the same ships we walked past yesterday. Yes, I'm the one who wanted to see the church up close. The front entrance features granite lions on both sides of the ornate entrance. The cathedral might be part of why I wanted to come here, but this view of the city is worth the walk alone.

Next to me, Lina admires the perspective from this higher elevation. It's taken a large part of my self-control to hold back the compliments I had when I saw her wearing the yellow sundress Chiara lent her for today. I bite the bullet and shift my gaze to hers. "You're so pretty it hurts. You know that Director Verde is smart to have sent a beautiful girl on that task. You're like my personal femme fatale."

"Funny, Maria said something about how sending me would leave you defenseless," she says.

"They missed a tiny detail, though…the girl always falls for the handsome prince," I flirt with a wink and receive an eye-roll in return. "All joking aside, do you want to go inside with me? I know many of the churches in Lazio look similar on the inside, but there's a comfort in knowing what to expect."

She nods and follows my lead into the sacred space. A glance around confirms that we're the only ones, but the quiet is tranquil rather than eerie. I silence my mind and reflect on the times my mother would teach me and Carlo about God and faith. When she passed away, the Christian faith traditions passed with her. Whether due to grief or never being on the same page as his wife, my father never engaged in anything religious unless it was connected to his position as king.

"When I have time to focus on something, I want to explore the Christian roots of this country," I whisper after several minutes of stillness. "It used to be a significant pillar of society, but we've lost the true meaning of it over the centuries. I don't want it to be a forced religion or anything; I think I want it to be real for people again. First, I need it to be real for me."

"We don't talk about it much at the Resistance, but elements of it are there," she says softly. "Deep down, I think we all want to know God and be known by Him. I think that's why it was so easy for me to lower my weapon at the possibility of not having to kill you. As much as I want to follow orders, I don't want to be responsible for taking the life of someone innocent. Most in the Resistance would be hesitant in the same position for the same convictions."

I give her a reassuring smile. "Well, I'm glad you didn't take me out as a way to attack my father. Getting rid of my family doesn't exactly mean you'd be getting rid of the monarchy as I'm sure some would prefer; however, unlike my father, I am open to striking a deal."

"ARE YOU READY?" I ask Franco as he walks into the living room, freshly showered and in an emerald green button-up shirt. He fidgets with the slim bracelet box in his hand, his nerves evident.

"You do know that asking her to be your girlfriend means that you're committing to just her, right?" Lina teases to help ease his jitters. She's back to reading *Jane Eyre* while waiting for dinner.

He gives her a sardonic expression. "If I recall, you were the one who suggested that I try to stick to one girl," he says. Then he utters to me, "You might want to watch that one. She speaks her mind a lot."

I grin and reply, "Just what I need."

Once Franco is out the door, I take the cooked lasagna out of the oven and carry the wine and candles outside. I set them in the center of the table I had set up outside when she was in the shower. A romantic candlelight dinner with a view of the sunset over the sea is the perfect backdrop to give her the necklace. I light the candles and jog back inside to cut the lasagna and transfer the steaming pieces to plates. Hearing my movement in the kitchen, Lina joins me.

"Anything I can do to help?" she asks me.

I hand her one of the plates and instruct, "Carry your plate and follow me."

"Carry my plate where?" she questions with an intrigued look. Rather than answer her, I guide her to the table outside. "When did you do this?" The wonder in her eyes and voice makes the planning I put into this worth it already.

"You take longer in the shower than I do," I tell her as I pull out her chair for her. After she sits, I gently push her closer to the table. When I sit down, I pour the wine into the glasses I had brought out earlier. "I started scheming as soon as Franco said we would have the place to ourselves."

"You set impossible standards for every other guy," she sighs. "I guess in the future I'll have to refer to you as 'the one who got away.'"

"This is simple stuff, Lina, and it's the early days. If a guy isn't willing to do little things like this in the beginning when the rose-colored glasses are on, he's not going to know how to love you and romance you when you have a life together and there are a million other distractions. This isn't me being larger than life; this is my way of showing you what you deserve. Adelina, I love you."

Her eyes water with tears that she attempts to blink away. "I love you, too, Prince Niccolò. As much as it goes against my inclination towards self-preservation, I love you." Hearing her voice say those words makes my heart soar. I take her hand in mine and kiss the soft skin.

"I hoped you would say that, though given how little time we've known each other, I would have understood if you hadn't. Now, let's eat and talk about things that won't make you almost cry." She laughs, and we eat the homemade recipe my mother had taught me.

"You know what's funny?" she says and eats the last bite of her lasagna before continuing to answer her rhetorical question. "I thought that I wouldn't get many home-cooked meals during this stint back to Venezia, but your cooking has been a pleasant surprise. Every part of you has been a pleasant surprise. More than pleasant."

I memorize the glow of her skin in the rosy hue of sunset. Both of us have likely made our fair share of assumptions about each other in this short time, which I aim to rectify. "Am I your first love?" I ask her hesitantly.

"Yes, but not the first one I've thought was attractive since I'm not blind," she elaborates. "Given the mission and my training and likely Dario's protectiveness, no one I was interested in ever reciprocated. Which was fine because I couldn't afford to be distracted. So before you ask, yes, you were my first kiss." Even in the fading light, I can see the blush on her face. "Am I your first love?"

"Lina, the past two weeks are the most social interaction I've had with anyone outside the castle in the last decade," I tell her. "What do you think?"

"You have castle staff, though. It's not unheard of for princes to have dalliances with pretty maids."

I shake my head as I say, "All castle staff is handpicked and paid by my father. I may not agree with him on much, but he emphasized the importance of the firstborn being a legitimate heir. He likely paid extra to ensure there would be no dalliances for me or my brother. Before my brother died, I kissed a girl or two, but it was not the way I kiss you. Yes, you are my first love. Sometimes I wonder if you'll be the only girl I love this way."

"Surely you'll love the Sozzini daughter," she whispers.

"In the kind of love that develops over time, it's likely. But in the soul-on-fire, all-consuming, magnetic-force kind of love, you're probably it for me," I tell her with certainty.

She leans back in her chair with a sigh. "I didn't think I would ever have this for the first time. And yet here you are insisting that I'll find someone who does things like this for me when you feel that you'll only have this once."

"Because the logical chances that she'll make me feel this way too are improbable," I explain to her. "I'm stuck with her, one person and no options. You have the freedom to search and wait until you find a connection like this again. Chemistry isn't as rare as you think, and I want you to have that with someone who can have a future with you. Loving you from a distance will be easier if you're happy."

"You think you'll love me even then?"

"I can't imagine I'll ever stop." The declaration leaves her speechless as the candlelight's shadows dance across her face. Feeling the necklace in my pocket, I brace for another risk. "I have something that I want to give you, but before I do, I need you to promise that you'll keep it. You're not allowed to throw it in the Venetian Lagoon or any other bodies of water or the trash."

She rolls her eyes at me and says, "I don't normally make promises about things without knowing the details first, but I'll make an exception for you."

"Stand up and close your eyes," I request. Lina shoots me a wry expression, but does what I ask. I stand and gently sweep her curls to one side over her shoulder. With the necklace in my hand, I put it around her neck, hooking the clasp in the back. Then I gently kiss the exposed skin below where her jaw meets her earlobe. I can hear when her breath hitches at my touch. I trail kisses down the slope of her neck to her shoulder.

"Throughout history, rubies have represented nobility, purity, and passion," she says when she opens her eyes and admires the gemstone.

When she turns around to look at me, I tell her, "As soon as I saw it, it reminded me of the first time we met."

"That was only a few weeks ago," she laughs as she admires the red reflection. "It does feel longer than that, though, doesn't it?"

"Time as a general construct seems to move differently since I met you."

We clean up our dishes and return the borrowed table and chairs to where I had found them. Once things are stored in their rightful place, we spend the rest of our time alone on the couch kissing, cuddling, and talking like the normal couple we aren't but wish we could be.

CHAPTER 9

Adelina

Chiara and Franco say their goodbyes with plans for her to visit Venezia next month. He must have disclosed his past to her for him to be comfortable with the idea of her coming to a city where his former dates stroll the streets. She doesn't strike me as the type to feel insecure about uncontrollable circumstances like that, though.

When I ask Franco if he minds that I sit in the back seat with Nic, he exclaims, "No way am I chauffeuring you two around while you make out in the back seat! You two can survive being a few feet away from each other for three and a half hours." Not wanting to upset our friend and driver, I claim the front passenger seat again. I pull down the visor to look at the necklace in the mirror's reflection, admiring the way it catches the sunlight. Broken heart or not, the ruby is too precious to throw away. He didn't need to make me promise to guarantee I would keep this.

"I'm going to miss the sea cliffside views," I sigh as we head north and inland toward Verona.

After a few moments of awkward silence, Nic says, "Verona is the city where the legend of Romeo and Giulietta takes place.

It's supposed to be romantic and architecturally similar to Venezia, but without the canals."

"There's nothing romantic about a double suicide," I can't resist quipping. At Nic's raised eyebrow, I elaborate. "First of all, the story is categorized as a tragedy. That alone should be telling and a warning. Secondly, Giulietta was only thirteen, which justifies why the whole thing was so dramatic, given that she was a teenage girl. I understand that it was a different time and culture in which it was common for girls to marry that young, but no thirteen-year-old should have to think about marriage or running away with her true love. The fact that they both die is due to suboptimal foresight and a lack of communication on both sides. Fate had nothing to do with both of them committing suicide. I do have sympathy regarding the star-crossed lovers aspect of having to go to extremes to have a life together. That, I do understand, even if they weren't doomed to fail in trying."

"In other words, at least one of them wasn't already betrothed to someone else?" Nic voiced the unspoken words of my rant. "I suspect a blood feud isn't much easier. You're right, though, about their deaths. If Romeo hadn't gone to the extreme of killing himself because he couldn't see a life without her, he might have been alive when she woke up. Ironically, his mindset that he couldn't live without her is what prevented their happy ending. Not that she chose any better when she woke up to find him dead. All that aside, Verona is still a romantic city."

Franco interjects, "Neither of you mentioned the fact that at the beginning of the story, Romeo thinks he's in love with Giulietta's cousin. It's as if the dude had a death wish to keep pursuing girls from the same forbidden family. At the time that they meet, he's there to try to see her cousin. Then he sees Giulietta, and it's suddenly love at first sight, like the other girl had never existed."

"I could see it on your face when you met Chiara," I say to Franco. "So clearly, love at first sight isn't that strange a notion."

"Same," Nic agrees from the back seat. "It was fairly obvious to both of us."

"What about you, Nic? When you saw Lina for the first time at the ball, what was going through your mind?" Franco asks.

I turn around so I can see his face better. Deep blue eyes meet mine as a heart-melting smile stretches across his mouth. Apart from the small scar on his right cheek, it's the same kind face that had helped me off the floor. "Never have I understood Romeo more than in that moment," he replies.

If we weren't in a moving car on the highway, I would crawl over the seat to kiss him. Maybe it was in that first moment that I decided I wouldn't be able to release my arrow when the time came. The way he looked at me as if I were the most captivating person in the room—it left me incapable of following through. For me, I wouldn't describe it as love at first sight, but more of a knowing that I could fall in love with him if given the opportunity.

Not only does Verona have visually aesthetic similarities to home, but it's also our last stop before the final stretch ending in Venezia. We meet our contacts at a restaurant with a view of the Adige River. Though it's not quite the same as eating lunch along the Canal Grando, Verona displays its unique type of beauty. Like our contacts in Lucera, we spend our lunch with another married couple here.

"Franco, how is your mother doing?" The wife, whose name

is Linda, asks him. "It's been too long since I've seen her. You were still a teenager the last time we visited Venezia."

"She's doing well," Franco tells her with a smile. Until now, I hadn't realized that Franco already knew our Verona contacts. "I'm sure she misses me right now, but I'll be home soon enough."

"And you're still unmarried," Linda states with some question in her voice. "A man like you should be able to find yourself a nice, pretty wife. Your mother isn't getting any younger, and I'm sure she would like to be alive to meet her grandchildren." These types of conversations have never been directed at me, though I've heard of other girls my age and younger receiving the same treatment. I don't have biological parents waiting around for me to give them grandchildren, though I'm sure Maria's parents would treat my children like their own descendants.

Franco blushes with a shrug. "I might have found a girl that I can see myself starting a family with. It's still too early to know, though," he admits sheepishly. The right woman can turn a self-proclaimed womanizer into a romantic fool.

Linda's husband, Andrea, must have sensed or noticed Nic's subtle touches on my hand and arm because he asks, "What about you, Lina? We have a saying that if you love someone, bring them to Verona. You and your friend here would make some handsome children." I feel the heat rush through my body as the blush overtakes my complexion. In my peripheral vision, I can see the redness on Nic's face, too. This mission coming to a close may also remove my immunity from such comments once I'm home.

"I haven't thought much about marriage or children," I admit to them without looking at Nic. "I've spent the last few years focused on training, which doesn't leave much time for extracurricular activities."

Linda chimes in, "From personal experience, it's usually when you're not planning for it that it suddenly falls in your lap."

We walk away from the restaurant, and I feel the same sense of relief I had the previous two times we met with Resistance contacts. Andrea and Linda hadn't shown any suspicion of Nic's fake name and story. As far as they know, my blooming romance is with an agent named Pasquale. The apartment set aside for our stay is a ten-minute drive from our lunch location. Fortunately, it has three bedrooms, allowing each of us to have privacy.

"Two bathrooms, though," Franco confirms after doing a quick inspection of the layout. "Nic and I have no problem sharing." Being the only female in our small group works to my advantage once again. The two flights of stairs between our car and the apartment are enough for the boys to let me carry my luggage this time. My muscles come alive with the exercise and elevated heart rate, making me miss the burn and soreness that accompany constant training. Nic and I create a list of items needed from the store based on what's already in the small kitchen.

"Another gelato trip?" Franco asks us when he sees the handwritten list that Nic is jotting down. The moment morphs into something bittersweet when I recognize that this will be our last first night in a new location. The next bedroom I sleep in after this one will be my own, filled with familiar comforts and a waiting sister, but far from Nic's warmth.

"Ice cream first," Nic agrees as he shoves the list in his pocket and interlaces his fingers in mine.

"Even though I know this was meant to be a tourist trap, it's still a nice attraction," I observe as we stroll the courtyard off Via Cappello. While there are still visitors buzzing their way in and out of the house, it's not the overwhelming crowds that once plagued this landmark. On the towering wall to our right is the infamous balcony protruding from the exterior of the house.

"That's not the only balcony in this courtyard," Nic muses beside me. "Giulietta must have been an introvert if she felt the need to escape to a balcony during a house party."

I look at him with a quizzical look on my face. "Are you an introvert or an extrovert? I know that you've spent much of your adult life secluded, but that wasn't by your own choice. Do you gain energy from being around others or from being by yourself?"

"Either, both," he shrugs. "If I were to pinpoint it on a scale, I would be close to the middle, but leaning more toward introverted. I'm guessing you're also introverted."

"Correct, but I do enjoy spending time with a few close friends," I smile, shifting my attention back to the courtyard. "I do like the way the vines have grown over the wall in a mix of architecture and nature. Nature has a way of surviving amid brick and stone."

"Are those—" Nic begins asking, but I interrupt him.

"Letters to Juliet," I finish for him. "People still do that." His expression is blank, inviting further explanation. "Women and maybe men with all sorts of relationship problems come here and leave a letter for Giulietta asking for advice. It's for those who have lost love or are lost in love. There are secretaries of Giulietta who respond to the letters left in that red letterbox. It's amazing to see how all this has evolved from two people who never actually existed."

"Lost in love," Nic repeats, musing over the phrase. I can see the idea forming in his mind, but no secretary is going to be able to give me sound advice regarding a love betrothed to another. It's not the type of "lost" that one finds their way out of.

Franco emerges from the gift shop with trinkets in tow. "I wonder whose idea it was to forge a bronze statue of a fictional underage girl?" Franco says it low enough that only Nic and I can hear.

"It's a replica of the original," I say to burst his bubble. "The original had to be replaced due to the legend surrounding the statue."

"Legend?" both boys question at the same time.

I tell them, "The legend says that if you rub the right breast of the statue, your love misfortunes will turn around. I would imagine that with enough people rubbing the right side, things would become uneven."

They exchange glances before walking over to the statue. Nic points at me and mouths, *This is for you*, before rubbing the bronze. Next, Franco also rubs the bronze breast despite his love lacking much misfortune compared to many others. They both look at me expectantly as if it were my turn to do the same. I shake my head.

"The way I see it," Franco starts in an attempt to convince me, "the two of you could use all the help you can get. Unless you've given up on having anything together once we leave Verona."

Despite my misgivings, I step up to the statue and imitate the two boys who had participated in the ritual before me, if only to satisfy them. "I think it's ridiculous, but if it keeps the two of you from teaming up against me," I say to them with a tight smile. "Do we want to go inside, or are we moving on from the factitious meeting place of the supposed star-crossed lovers?"

Nic shakes his head with a smile, but Franco eyes me in disbelief. "For a girl who's in love, you're not nearly as dramatically romantic as most females in that situation. Maria would be fascinated by all of this if she were here with Dario."

I shrug, unable to argue with his accurate assessment. Nic adds, "Of the two of us, I think I'm the hopelessly romantic one the majority of the time. She's typically the one trying to keep herself grounded and realistic, which isn't a bad thing. In a way, we've been taking turns being the voice of logic and forethought. One of us has to keep both of us from doing something stupid."

"Maria and I are very different people, too," I say. "It's why she and Dario complement each other so well. Plus, their relationship has been slow, steady, and meant to last from the start. No situations or external circumstances to pull them apart. It's so…normal."

The three of us walk back out onto one of the main streets to find a restaurant for lunch. Nic whispers in my ear, "Do you envy the effortlessness of Dario and Maria's love?"

Blue eyes probe mine as I affirm, "I envy nothing when compared to what I have with you."

"Do you think Franco stayed behind to write letters for Chiara, or do you think he's grown tired of being the third wheel?" Nic asks me as we cross the bridge in the direction of the gardens.

"Likely both," I guess, not sorry about the alone time we've been granted. "These gardens are supposed to be more romantic than Giulietta's house, so I don't blame him for wanting to pass on accompanying us. Part of him probably pities us more and more each day."

"I wish we had more time," he whispers as we approach the Giardino Giusti. Cypress trees line the perimeter of the infamous labyrinth. The various sculptures of Olympic gods that are scattered throughout the maintained petite hedges of the "Leave in Trench" area of the garden are absent in this section. When we reach one end, Nic instructs me, "Stay here," as he jogs around to the opposite end.

"What are you doing?" I ask with amusement.

He continues his journey and says, "The local legend claims that lovers who manage to find each other in the labyrinth are destined to be together."

"Nic." I'm growing weary of local legends that are meant to give false hope to couples like us.

"Humor me, please," he responds, now at the other end. This maze is child's play compared to navigating the streets of Venezia or the passageways of the castle. We find each other easily, his arms sweeping me into his embrace when we meet. Before I can complain about the simplicity of the endeavor, his lips silence my words and thoughts. It's an ever-effective method to render me speechless. Without others around to interrupt, we savor the moment. We venture through other parts of the garden, including the grotto and tower at the back end. If I hadn't already fallen for his blue eyes or heart-stopping smile, I would have fallen for him here. It's as magical a place as Piasa San Marco at sunrise or sunset with its romantic atmosphere.

It's when we're adrift in the mid-afternoon sunlight that Franco finds us, a solemn expression on his face.

"Franco, what's wrong?" I ask as my stomach drops. He would only be here if there's bad news.

"Director Verde is waiting for you at the apartment. She sent me to come get you—both of you," he relays apologetically. Nic's grip around my waist tightens as the repercussions of his words sink in. Our planned week in Verona is being cut short by three days. Three days less with Nic than we had thought. As soon as we set foot in the apartment, this is over.

"Give us a few minutes, and we'll catch up," Nic requests of Franco, who obliges with a sad smile before heading back to the apartment. Nic's warm hands are on the sides of my face as his lips frantically and passionately move against mine. It's a kiss to communicate a lifetime of goodbyes crammed into the present. I can feel the tears trickle down my cheeks as he wordlessly reminds me of the vastness of his love for me. When he notices my crying, his lips leave mine to kiss away the tears from my cheeks, but I don't stop the tears that brim in his own eyes. "I love you, Adelina," he whispers into my hair as he hugs me tight against him. "Never forget and never doubt how much."

"And I love you, Niccolò," I say into his chest. "For every second of the rest of my life."

Before I'm ready—because I will never be prepared—we walk back to the apartment, our hands holding each other's for our last day together like this.

CHAPTER 10

Niccolò

If Lina is nervous about the impending and unexpectedly early meeting, it doesn't show in her posture. This is her world that we're about to step into, a world where I'm the clear outsider. She squeezes my hand in reassurance before letting go to open the apartment door.

All eyes are on us as the door swings open. The woman, whom I can only assume is Director Verde, carries authority and confidence in a way similar to my father. With Franco and her are two other male Resistance agents, both of whom Lina knows.

"Dario!" she proclaims with excitement toward the blond man. Despite the current circumstances, he gives her a quick, friendly hug.

I gauge where this will lead and what this will mean for me and my plans. Neither of the agents is glaring at me, nor have they arrested me or restrained me. I assume it would be easy enough to kill me if they wanted to do so, given how outnumbered I am. Then again, if it comes down to a physical brawl, would Lina fight with the Resistance, or would she step in to defend me? While there is tension in the air, it's not as bad as it should be if they see me as the enemy. Director Verde scrutinizes me, but her brown eyes don't show hatred or disgust—interest and curiosity are the dominant emotions I sense.

"Sorry to cut your stay here short, but the prince's presence changes the timeline," Zeta Verde says in a commanding tone. She doesn't yell, but her voice carries a firmness that discourages any argument. "Lina and Franco, you'll be traveling back to the city with Leandro and me. Dario, you're to take the prince back to your apartment for the night and bring him to the base at eight tomorrow morning. Lina, I also expect you in my office at eight tomorrow for a debriefing. Pack your things."

That's it. No explanation as to why our time here has been cut short or what awaits us in the morning. Lina whispers something to Dario that I can't hear, and he nods in agreement to her statement or request. I look at Lina and give her a small smile before we disappear into our rooms to gather our luggage. Dario follows me and stands in the doorway, inspecting me with the same curiosity that the Director had. Given his apparent position within the Resistance and in Lina's life, I know that I need him on my side.

"SHOULD I assume it's a good thing I'm still alive and not in restraints?" I tentatively ask the brother figure Lina had told me so much about. I've grown so accustomed to Franco's friendly demeanor that Dario's seems hostile in comparison. His posture in the driver's seat is less relaxed than Franco's, but at least I get to occupy the front passenger seat for the ride.

"I don't know much," Dario admits, his eyes fixed on the road heading to Venezia. "A few days after the ball, Director Verde informed me that you hadn't been found dead. A week after that, she received word that you were traveling with Lina and Franco. It's hard to tell, but to me, she didn't seem surprised at either set of news. I'm just following her orders, but it appears that she's treating you as a guest rather than a prisoner."

My mind races at the possibilities, but one worry takes precedence above the others. "Will anything happen to Lina for not obeying orders?" I nearly beg with my question, even though Dario isn't the one who decides.

"I think she'll be fine," Dario says with quasi-certainty. "Director Verde has always had a soft spot for Lina. It bodes well that she's going home tonight to rest rather than straight to the base for interrogation. And as I said, the director isn't surprised. Some details are going on above my clearance level. Maybe we'll finally get some answers at the meeting tomorrow."

The tension I've been holding in my body visibly relaxes knowing that she's safe. The hardness in Dario's jaw softens a bit at my reaction to his assurances. *Perceptive* is one of the words Franco had used to describe all Resistance agents, and that trait will either help or hurt my chances of gaining Dario's favor.

"You love her, don't you?" he asks softly. "I thought I saw something in the way you looked at her. You're worried about her, probably more than you're worried for yourself."

"I don't know what I would do if something happened to her, especially if it were my fault," I say in admission.

Dario's resigned expression is similar to what I've recognized on Franco's face a few times over the last few weeks. "Please tell me she's not pregnant."

"I would never risk putting her in that position," I say to him.

"Well then, I like you a bit more already," Dario concedes. "Seemingly, Franco likes you, too. Most importantly, Lina likes you, and her discernment with people is typically fairly sharp. Which means you must be a good guy, especially since you say you didn't sleep with her. You are more like your mother, aren't you?"

Being compared to my mother is a high compliment considering the reputation of my living parent. "If you were to ask my father, he would say I'm too much like her," I murmur with a wry smile. Dario laughs at my response.

Enthusiastically, this time, he adds, "And you love Lina. I noticed the gold and ruby necklace she was wearing, and I'm guessing that was a gift from you. If she's willing to accept jewelry from you, she loves you. She doesn't accept gifts lightly." I take a deep breath, hoping Dario will still sympathize once he knows the whole story.

"I'm also betrothed, thanks to my parents, to someone whose family disappeared when I was only two," I tell him with unhidden disdain. "A betrothal that my father tried to hide away from me in the royal records. I'm legally tied to a family who fled the country because of him. Long story short, Director Verde is a cousin of the family and the only one who might know how I can find my betrothed, assuming she's alive."

"You're in love with Lina, but you're betrothed to someone else," Dario says with full understanding. "How legally binding are betrothals in Lazio? I've never heard of those still happening before now."

"I might as well be engaged, but without my promise or ring on her finger. Technically, the only way out is if one of us dies and there's proof of death."

Dario is somber at my explanation. "Did Lina know all this from the beginning?"

"I told her on the night after we left the castle. Right after, I stopped her from almost kissing me." At this, Dario's eyebrows raise in surprise.

"She initiated it? We're talking about the same Lina, right?"

"Unless she has a twin I don't know about," I respond with a shrug.

The car is silent as Dario wrestles through all the tangles in this web. "She's going to hate me for saying this, but I don't think it's a good idea for you to see Lina until tomorrow morning," he explains to me. "Once we're at my place and you're settled, I can check on her. I'll need you to promise that you won't leave my apartment if I leave you alone for an hour."

"You have my word," I swear to him. "Even if I did leave, I don't know my way around Venezia. Based on what I've heard from Franco and Lina, it doesn't sound like the easiest city to navigate, particularly for a newcomer."

Dario chuckles. "It will be nearly impossible for you without a map. Lina, on the other hand, can find her way around blindfolded. I can't take you to her, but I can't stop her from coming to see you if she chooses to do so."

As much as I want that—more time, more kisses, more of the electricity and fire that inundates through my being when I'm around her—more of anything will only make it harder for both of us. "Tell her that I think it would be better if she doesn't try to see me tonight," I struggle to say. "She might be strong enough, but I don't think I am. I can only handle saying goodbye to her so many times before it breaks me."

Dario nods with a sad smile. "She's a survivor. Maria and I will make sure she gets through this."

"I'm glad she has you," I tell him genuinely. "I want her to remember me as someone who loves her, not as someone who broke her heart. Speaking of Maria, tell me about her, from your perspective." The heaviness in the car lifts as Dario spills about the love of his life. Though his words and descriptions of her and how she makes him feel sound familiar to my thoughts about Lina, the details are unique to their story and relationship. I distract myself from my looming future by listening to Dario talk about his upcoming wedding.

"By the way, how should I address you?" Dario asks. "Is it 'Your Highness' or 'Prince Niccolò'?"

I chuckle and say, "My friends call me Nic."

CHAPTER 11

Adelina

True to her word in the Verona apartment, Director Verde doesn't question me on the car ride to Tronchetto, the furthest into the lagoon that cars can go. Perhaps she wants to be able to completely focus on me when I give her a detailed account of what happened the night of the ball. Right now, she silently sits in the front passenger seat as Leandro drives and Franco and I share the backseat. If she's angry, it doesn't show through her cool expression. I had been expecting her anger when I walked in with the prince. Rather than kill him on the spot or put him in restraints, she simply separated us by ordering Dario to escort him to Venezia in the car Franco, Nic, and I had been traveling back in. Nic is also staying with Dario tonight, not in a holding cell.

Halfway through the drive, Director Verde asks Franco, "I trust that you weren't followed leaving the castle grounds, correct?"

"Correct," Franco confirms without further explanation. His hands fidget as he waits for her response.

"Good," she says with a small smile. "As far as our sources can tell, the king still believes the prince is at the family villa in Napoli. However, Rafael recognized him as well as Andrea and Linda. We couldn't take any chances that someone with loyalties to the king, who knows what he looks like, identifies him in a place other than Napoli." At least that explains the impromptu end to our stay in Verona. Except that this is the woman who meticulously planned and trained me for years to assassinate the prince whom she now has no issue helping hide from the king.

I should wait until tomorrow to ask the question that eats away at my calm demeanor, but I won't sleep tonight if I don't hear an answer sooner. "Why don't you seem upset or angry that I didn't follow your orders to kill him?" I ask her, but my question is met with silence.

From what I can gather in the reflection of the car's mirrors, her body language is contemplative. We park in a small lot on Tronchetto designated for the Resistance fleet and walk to the pier to continue our journey to the main city by boat. Leandro helps Franco move our luggage over when Director Verde motions for me to join her on board while we wait. I sit next to her per her wordless instructions.

"Do you know why you're my best agent?" she asks me in a tone that leaves me unsure whether or not she means for it to be rhetorical. I shake my head in case she expects a response. "Your instincts about situations and people have always been spot on. You possess the uncanny ability to make correct judgment calls on a person's character with very little interaction with them. I saw it when we tested you by showing you short videos of both Resistance allies and the king's allies. You're the only agent who has scored perfectly on that examination in all the years I've been head of the Resistance.

"That's the skill I needed most from you going into this mission. I sent you with full confidence that you would make the right choice, whether to kill the prince or spare his life. Of all the intel I and other agents could gather, the one thing we couldn't be sure of is the type of king the prince will become. If he had been like his father or worse, you would have followed through without a doubt. But given that he's not only alive, but also has been traveling with you and Franco for weeks, he must not be an enemy to us or to those who want what's good for the kingdom. So no, Lina, I'm not angry or upset; you did what I hoped you would do. You followed your instincts and spared the life of an innocent prince."

I stare off into the water, allowing her words to sink in. I had been preparing myself for the worst-case scenario regarding Director Verde. As much as the compliments intertwined within her elaboration should have settled my worries, I still have questions without logical answers. My eyes shift back to hers as I ask, "You're not even upset that I brought him here?"

"I am a bit curious as to why he willingly left the castle and joined you and Franco for that roundabout trip, but I was going to wait until tomorrow morning to ask him myself," she admits to me.

"He wants to talk to you," I tell her, "to ask you about your cousin Valentina and her daughter."

I don't miss the flash of recognition that crosses her face at the mention of her cousin. "Tomorrow," Director Verde insists as Franco and Leandro join us on the boat.

Tomorrow. At least tonight I can rest knowing I haven't led Nic into a death trap.

I'm feet away from the front door of the place I call home when the entrance springs open, and Maria is running to embrace me. The familiar warmth of my sister's hug breaks some of the defenses I had constructed to hold myself together until I reach my bedroom. My parents also rush out to greet me with hugs and kisses. My eyes brim with tears of joy and relief at reunification with my family.

"Dario told us he was going with Director Verde to bring you home today, so Mama cooked all of your favorites for dinner tonight," Maria tells me as we walk to our shared room. Once we're out of earshot of our parents, she asks me, "Lina, what's going on? I thought you wouldn't be home for another few days, and Dario was acting strange when he told me he would be going to Verona today."

I lie down on my bed and stare up at the ceiling. "I didn't assassinate the prince," I relay to her, and I hear her loud sigh of relief.

"Lina, it's going to be okay," she tries to encourage me. "I know that it was the point of all the training and everything, but you're not a killer. It never sat well with me that Director Verde wanted him dead."

"She doesn't, though. Unbeknownst to me, my job was to assassinate the prince only if he was like his father. Director Verde anticipated that I would spare him if I discerned that he's good and innocent."

"Well, isn't it good news that the crown prince isn't the ruthless man his father is? And how does that explain what happened in Verona today?" Maria sits on the floor next to my bed, taking my hand nearest her in her own. It's a gesture of reassurance she reserves for when I've had a hard day.

I turn my body to face her, and her eyes shift to the ruby pendant around my neck. Maria gasps at the reflective red gem. "Did the prince give that to you?" I nod my head, swallowing back the tears threatening to invade my resolve. "Tell me everything." And I do. I start with the night of the ball and how the few hours I spent in the grand ballroom felt like a fairytale. Bittersweet tears fall as I recall the memories of the doomed love story.

"Half the time I'm with him, I forget that he's the next king of Lazio," I whisper to her. "Kissing him goodbye earlier today was the hardest thing I've ever had to do."

Maria strokes my hair as she consoles me, "I told you that you would leave him defenseless. I can't imagine how hard it must have been for both of you today. If he's staying with Dario, maybe we can go see him tonight, if you want."

"He doesn't want you to come," Dario's voice says from the doorway, a sad expression on his face. He kneels beside my bed next to Maria. "He doesn't think he can handle saying goodbye to you again. You just had to make a prince fall in love with you, didn't you?" He jokes to try to lighten my mood, and I give him a small smile for the gesture.

Now that Dario is here with us, I feel slightly better. Maria says, "Also, are you serious about Franco committing to one girl without sleeping with her? We're talking about the same guy, right?"

Dario chimes in, "I thought I was mishearing when Nic told me the same thing."

I smile a little bigger as I note, "He told you to call him Nic. That means you like him and he likes you."

"He's not the spoiled, insufferable royal I was expecting," Dario admits with a shrug. "And it's hard to find fault with a guy who's as protective of you as I am. That doesn't mean I approve of the fact that you've been running around canoodling with him, but at least he assured me that you're not carrying his child."

I sit up and glare at Dario. "This is me we're talking about. Do you honestly think I would let myself be in that type of dead-end situation?"

Dario's expression softens. "I think that you have a lot of intense feelings for him, and it's not always easy to make sound decisions when you're falling in love. But it sounds like you two at least did the right thing when it came to that."

Maria pipes up, "But seriously, what is Franco's girlfriend like?"

Glad to change the topic away from Nic, I update them on Chiara and the time we spent with her in Ancona. After he's certain I'm okay, Dario returns to his apartment to relay my condition to Nic. Maria and I eat dinner and dessert with our parents. Unlike Maria, they don't pry into all the details of my early return, but keep their questions on topics such as the various cities we stayed in and what the castle is like. When I curl up in my bed for the night, sleep comes quickly, but my dreams are invaded by sets of blue eyes and Director Verde's dark ones.

CHAPTER 12

Niccolò

"I know this seems extreme, but for security reasons, I'm going to need to blindfold you until we reach the base," Dario tells me as I finish getting ready for my meeting with Director Verde.

"I guess I'll just have to trust that you wouldn't lead me into a death trap after your hospitality last night," I joke, waiting for him to tie the strip of cloth in his hand around my head. He does so in a way that's secure without being too uncomfortable. Dario expertly communicates and leads me from his apartment to the Resistance base. There are too many stairs, twists, and turns for my brain to memorize the path, and without my eyesight, I don't have landmarks to use as a guide. I don't ask whether he's following orders by doing this or if it's for his amusement. Eventually, I hear the beeps of passcodes being entered into keypads, a clear indication that we're passing through secure doorways. Once we're inside, he removes the blindfold and gives me time to adjust my eyes to the light.

I follow him through a maze of hallways that are likely a reflection of the city streets until he knocks on a door before opening it. Inside is an office with emerald walls, fitting given

Verde's last name. Director Verde sits behind a white desk and gestures for me to sit in the only remaining empty chair, the other chair on this side of the desk already occupied by Lina. Dario closes the door behind him as he leaves the three of us alone. I resist the urge to reach out and touch Lina to reassure her.

"I trust that you both slept well," Director Verde says, making small talk. She doesn't strike me as the type to beat around the bush, though, making her statement seem uncharacteristic. Both of us nod slightly, unsure of whether to speak. "Prince Niccolò, I feel I should catch you up on some of what I discussed with Lina on the journey back from Verona yesterday. I hope you see that I have no intentions of harming you, even though I sent an assassin to your ball. As I explained to Lina, I entrusted her with that mission, knowing that if she saw good in you, she would spare your life. I wanted that to be the case, given my family's friendship with your mother. I'm glad to see that you take after her in many of the important ways."

I lean back in my chair, allowing the relief to permeate my emotions. It's one thing to suspect and assume she holds no ill will towards me, but it's another to hear her confirm it. In all this tangled web, I hadn't considered Zeta Verde's possible amicability with my mother.

The director continues by asking, "Lina, can you confirm that the prince left the castle of his own volition without your help or coercion?"

"That's correct," Lina confirms, the sound of her voice soothing my nerves. "When I spoke to him in his chamber, he was already packed and had plans to leave the castle that same night."

"Prince Niccolò, why were you trying to leave the castle, especially that late at night after your birthday celebration?" Verde directs her question at me.

I tell her about my discovery of the betrothal documents and how, when I searched for information regarding the Sozzinis in the castle records and archives, I was met with a dead end. Then, I fast-forward to my mother's journals and the note she left behind for me, written in code, that listed Zeta Verde's name. Finally, I explain that Lina and Franco were trying to help me by bringing me back with them.

"No, that was smart of them," Verde agrees. "By traveling with them, you remained undetectable to your father, and I appreciate that we managed to get you here without leaving a trail for him to follow. I suspected that you would show up here one day."

"Do you know where they are and how I can find them?" I finally ask her, bracing myself for all the possible answers I've mulled over for weeks.

The smile on Verde's face is unreadable, but it's there. It expresses a plethora of emotions—sadness, hope, and possibly pride. "I only know of the location of their daughter, the one you're betrothed to. As far as I've been able to find, Alessandro and Valentina didn't survive. Did any of the documents you found mention the first name of the heir to the Sozzini family line?"

"No, not even the announcement of her birth," I reply. The entire time, I've had to refer to her as something else due to the lack of information on her first name.

"Alessandro and Valentina removed as many records as they could before they tried to flee to make it harder for your father to find her," Director Verde explains. "It would have been simpler for you had you known from the start. Her name is Adelina Paxe."

I hear when Lina's breath catches at the revelation, and I watch Verde's eyes shift to look at her cousin's daughter sitting next to me. Duchess Adelina Sozzini of the House of Sozzini, the first daughter of Alessandro and Valentina Sozzini, is not only alive and well, but she's the same as my Lina. *My Lina.* All those times I tried to hold back my feelings for her. All the times I kissed her and told her that I love her. All the times I dreaded saying goodbye, she was always supposed to be mine. From before I laid eyes on her for the first time on my twenty-fifth birthday, she was meant to be my bride. At least, that's the first time that I remember seeing her.

Lina gets up from her chair and moves faster than I can stop her. She's already out the door by the time I stand to follow her, but Director Verde stops me, "Wait, give her some time to process this. I need to talk to you alone."

I say the first thing that comes to my mind, "You sent my betrothed to make a life-or-death judgment call on my character?"

She winces at my accusation. "I sent her because she's gifted at discerning people. But yes, I believed that whether or not you were aware of your connection, it would help her make the right decision. I couldn't have predicted that you would fall in love with each other, though, at least, not this quickly. That had nothing to do with my intentions and everything to do with the choices you two have made since you met. And I needed her to meet you before I told her the truth about everything."

I chose to kiss Lina, to let myself love Lina, because it's something I want, not because of the legally binding contract. If anything, not knowing it's been her the whole time slowed down the inevitable. Or perhaps not knowing is what made her more open to me to begin with. Director Verde slides a thick piece of paper across her desk to me. My heart stops when I see the well-forged death certificate for Adelina Paxe Sozzini.

"I'm not saying you shouldn't marry her," Director Verde explains softly. "In fact, in training her, I always kept that possibility in mind. I wanted her to be prepared if she does marry you, because we still haven't been able to uncover proof of why your father wants her dead. Marrying you is a risk, but it's one she's capable of handling. I'm giving this to you because you both deserve to make the choice. If you choose to marry her and she chooses to marry you, you have my blessing and support."

Knowing I'm unlikely to have a private meeting with her like this again, I ask, "Can you tell me about the Sozzinis?" Zeta Verde obliges and shares all she knows from before and after Adelina's birth, focusing on the changes that led to her sudden fleeing with her cousin's baby daughter.

Adelina

ario tries to stop me on my flight out of the base, but with Nic still inside Director Verde's office, he's obligated to stay behind with the prince. I use that to my advantage to get a head start—to discover a place to hide that will give me at least a few hours uninterrupted before Dario finds me. The bell tower in the Campanile di San Marco is easily accessible via elevator and too prominent, given its proximity to my favorite area of the city. The Scala Contarini del Bovolo is less obvious and not one of the places I usually frequent. The spiral staircase with its multiple arches is the type of architecture one would imagine for a fairytale tower. Ignoring the burn in my legs and heaviness in my lungs, I sprint up the stairs until I see the panoramic views of the Venetian rooftops. It's in that breathless moment that I allow Director Verde's words to sink in.

My parents are likely dead. It isn't a new revelation to me, but hearing their names, knowing who they are, brings my grief to the surface again. They loved me. Alessandro and Valentina Sozzini undoubtedly loved me. In their last attempt to keep me safe, they left me with Zeta Verde and the Resistance. Director Verde is my mother's cousin—my first cousin once removed, to be precise. Even though we're family, I know her favoritism towards me isn't based on that alone; she's not the only one to have praised my skills over the years. I feel slightly betrayed that she sent me on that mission that would force me to meet and possibly kill my betrothed, but there's no one else she could have sent. It always had to be me at that ball in the castle.

As the heir to the Sozzini estate, I'm technically a duchess. I've spent my whole life seeing myself as a commoner who happens to possess the skillset to be an extraordinary agent. Unbeknownst to me before today, I have a title—a high title at that. And I'm betrothed to the crown prince of Lazio, a marriage that would make me a princess and eventual queen. All this time, I thought I had a choice about what my future after the mission could look like, but now I'm just as bound to the things I was born into as Nic is. I'm the girl whom the king likely tried to kill as a baby.

The man I love, the embodiment of everything I want, is betrothed to me. Nic is the one my deceased parents wanted me to marry, and I'm the girl his mother trusted would be a good match for him, someone he couldn't help but love.

I stare out at the living, breathing city below me, staying far enough away from the railing to keep myself hidden from anyone who might look up from the courtyard below. If Dario wants to find me, he'll climb the staircase. Though every nook, cranny, canal, and bridge of the expanse around me is familiar, it doesn't hold the same sentiment of home as it had before I left. It's beautiful, but now I'm certain it's not the only beautiful place in the kingdom. I see the blond of Dario's hair before the rest of him appears at the top of the last set of stairs. He sits down next to me on the floor where the hallway meets the dome on the highest story.

"Your grace," he greets me, and I lightly punch him in the arm for addressing me as such. "I would like to point out that you chose the tower in Venezia that looks the most like it's from a fairytale to hide from a prince. Ironic, if you ask me."

"Correction, I chose the tower based on the fact that I've been hiding from you and knew where you would search first," I say to him. "The prince doesn't know his way around the city well enough to find me without the help of a local guide. I'm assuming he's waiting somewhere nearby, given your new role as his escort."

"He and Maria both are in the courtyard below, and Franco is on his way," Dario admits. "All of us are worried about you."

"My dead parents legally signed me away to a prince before I was even born," I say out loud.

"It sounds to me like both of your mothers were trying to find a way to unite your families officially," he tries to offer as solace. "You're not the only one whose deceased mother signed you into a marriage. His mother did the same. And in their defense, none of them could have known that he would become the heir apparent."

"He's a prince," I repeat out loud, more to myself than to my friend.

Dario chuckles at my statement. "He's always been a prince, the whole time, from the start of this. When you kissed him, he was a prince. When you told him you love him and accepted that necklace you're wearing, he was a prince. You've known from the beginning who you were falling in love with. The only thing that's changed is what happens from here. If you ask me, this should make things simpler for you."

"His father likely murdered my parents," I say deadpan. "I wouldn't call that simple."

"Lina, you were in tears last night at the thought of a life without him. If you love him, you won't let something like his title or his father get in the way. Anyway, I'm not the one you should be talking to about this. Are you ready to talk to him?"

"As ready as I'll ever be," I relent. Dario whistles loudly as a signal to Nic and starts heading down the staircase he ascended to reach the peak.

My nerves pick up as I watch and wait for him. Time moves both fast and slow. He's so familiar, the way he climbs the stairs, the way his blue eyes search my face. He sits next to me in the same spot Dario had vacated. Neither of us speaks as he catches his breath from the exertion; he must have sprinted up here the same way I had hours ago. We both stare out through the stone railings rather than at each other.

"It would seem that I've tracked down the woman my mother intended for me to marry," he says to break the silence.

"If you want to be technical, she tracked you down," I quip as I try to hide how fast my heart is racing.

"She almost made me beg for a dance at my birthday party. I should have known what I was getting myself into. The name 'Adelina' means 'nobility,'" he adds, "you'd think we would have caught that clue."

I reply, "Well, at least that makes sense."

I hear the deep breath he takes before he hands me a piece of paper he had folded up in his pocket. My eyes stare at a forged death certificate with my birth name on it, a way out. "You deserve to have a choice," he explains to me. "Asking you to leave the only life you've known and the only family you've had is a lot. Becoming a princess, queen, and mother to an heir is a lot to ask of anyone. I don't take lightly what I'm asking of you, and I am asking, Lina. But before you make a decision, you need to know the pros as well as the cons."

"You made a pros and cons list for me?" I laugh as I look at his beautiful face, the light scar on his cheek nearest to me. The scar from the night he stood up for me at the club. Finally, he looks at me, his blue eyes as vibrant as I've ever seen them.

"I would do whatever it takes," he replies with a shrug and a smile that would trip me up if I were doing anything but sitting. "But that's not one of my points. Firstly, I'm incredibly handsome and charming—arguably irresistible." I laugh as I shake my head in amusement. "Secondly, I'm a pretty good cook, which some would say is a very sexy quality in a man. Thirdly, and most important of all, I'm already madly, irreversibly in love with you. Finding that kind of love isn't always a guarantee for people in our position."

I blush at his declaration as my eyes drift back to the certificate in my hands. Quietly, I say, "I don't know whether or not I'll be able to give you an heir."

"What do you mean?" he asks in confusion.

Meeting his eyes again, I voice one of the worries that had presented itself in my mind while I sat here and pondered the future. "In the journals your mother left behind for you to read, my mother struggled to conceive before she had me. What if the source of her infertility is genetic, and I have the same problems? There's a chance I may never be able to give you a son or daughter."

"I'd rather have you than a dozen children," he insists as he holds my hands in his. "Plus, the process of trying for an heir with you sounds rather appealing to me. It wouldn't be the end of the world if we can't have children. There are others within the royal bloodline who are capable of ruling after me."

I search his eyes, confident in the sincerity of his words. Then, I do the only thing I deem appropriate—I rip up the fake death certificate until it's in too many pieces to reassemble.

He watches the mess of paper as I gather the pieces into a pile to be thrown away. Nic stands up first before helping me up, a smile plastered to his visage.

"It would appear that you're stuck with me," he says as he tosses the remnants of the death certificate into a nearby bin. "And just in time, too."

I resist the urge to ask and ruin whatever surprise he has planned. Hand in hand, we descend the spiral, a prince and his soon-to-be princess—a warrior princess. Our three friends greet us when we reach the courtyard, and Maria pulls me into a hug.

"We'll talk later," she whispers in my ear before releasing me.

Wherever Nic plans to take me, Dario, Maria, and Franco must be in on it too, since they walk in front of us as his guides. Though I know where we are and the direction we're headed, I'm still unsure what to expect. The golden rays of late afternoon fade into sunset as we approach the Piasa San Marco.

"I wanted to see your favorite spot at sunset with you," Nic explains as we stop in the middle of the bustling square. Maria, Dario, and Franco wander off somewhere nearby to give us privacy.

"What do you think of my city, Prince Niccolò?" I ask him as I breathe in the air as if it were magic.

He smiles at me. "Almost as breathtaking as you."

I turn to look at him and tease him for his cheesy line, but he's no longer standing beside me. Nic kneels on one knee while holding up a gold and ruby engagement ring. Nearby, I can hear the floating notes of a violin playing my favorite lullaby. "Adelina Paxe Sozzini, I've been in love with you since the moment I met you, and time has only made me more certain of that. It feels like a dream that I even get to ask you this. Will you marry me?"

"You make it impossible to say no," I answer as I take the ring from his hands and slip it onto my ring finger. When he's standing again, I pull him in for a kiss, our first kiss since learning I'm his betrothed. With his arms firmly around me, he spins me. In the distance, I hear the claps and cheers of our audience, which includes our friends.

With his eyes glued to mine, he asks, "Does the ring fit? It was my mother's, and I've been carrying it around with me for weeks."

Dumbfounded, I say, "Yes, but why did you buy me a necklace that matches this ring when you didn't know you would be proposing to me?"

"Because I didn't think you would ever find out," he admits without looking me in the eye. "Because giving you a necklace that looks like my mother's ring was the closest thing to it that I could give you at the time. And because, coincidentally, it really does remind me of when we met. Any other questions?"

As I think for a few seconds, the music fills the emptiness. "Is this song also a coincidence?"

With a puzzled expression, he explains, "My mother used to sing me this song when I couldn't fall asleep as a child."

"I have a faint memory of mine doing the same. It's always been my favorite." I smile at the thought of both our mothers humming the same lullaby to us, yet another small detail to connect us. "Are we eating dinner here? I'm starving."

When he gives me the choice to have dinner just the two of us or with our friends, I choose the latter. My time here has a limit once again, but I have a whole lifetime to eat dinner with Nic.

"It would seem that you two aren't star-crossed lovers after all. It must be because we rubbed the breasts," Franco says.

"I don't know about that since his father still tried to kill me," I argue, stifling a smile at the mention of the bronze statue in Verona.

Nic adds, "I think of it more as inevitable lovers, like a collision of destiny." A collision is accurate, literally. "But yes, Franco, it's definitely because we touched Giulietta's bosom." Nic winks, and Maria and Dario share a puzzled expression.

"What are you going to do about the king?" Maria asks us. "I can't imagine he would take too kindly to your engagement to the girl whose parents he murdered."

Blue eyes fixed on me again, Nic asks, "How soon can we marry? Is two weeks enough time?" A fortnight is hardly enough time to prepare anything, although it would be enough time for the bare minimum required.

Dario is the one who offers a response. "Two weeks will be enough." My best friend is certain, and Maria agrees with him. This isn't going to be just any wedding, though; it's the crown prince and his betrothed—a daughter born and raised in Venezia, a high-level Resistance agent, and a duchess. While I have my doubts about whether two weeks is enough time for what is sure to be a grand affair, I know the rush is necessary. Marriage to his son will add a layer of protection for me against the king when I come forward as a Sozzini. We are running low on time before Nic is expected back at the castle, and I can only go with him sharing his name, if even then.

As our group starts to head in separate directions to our various homes, Nic kisses me again. "It's not the boobs, but the garden maze that did it. Two weeks and then you're mine for the night, every night," he promises me, making me glad that a fortnight is enough time.

Maria waits until Dario and Nic are far out of earshot to delight, "Lina, you're going to be a princess. You're getting married to a swoon-worthy prince. You'll be a wife before I am."

"Oh, Maria, I wasn't trying to beat you to the altar," I say apologetically. "When I woke up this morning, I had no idea that it would end with a ring on my finger. It's the last thing I expected to happen."

"You mean you didn't wake up expecting to find out you're the long-lost daughter of a Duke who is the daughter also betrothed to the very prince you've been pining over?" she asks sarcastically. "You're right, it does sound too good to be true. We have so much that we need to get done if we're going to pull this off."

I point out to her, "I'm not the one who insisted that two weeks is enough time."

"It will be enough!" she firmly assures me as we walk into the home where we grew up together to tell our parents the news.

THE BASE IS quiet and empty before sunrise, making it the ideal time to work out in the secluded gym without interruption. Sleep was hard to come by after yesterday's events, so I slipped out of my bedroom and made the trek to my second home. The familiar burn as I push my muscles to their limit helps keep my thoughts from racing at light speed. Even this is something I'll miss—the rigidity and regularity it brought to my schedule. How does one go from intense physical training six days a week to being the prince's new bride?

"I should have known you would be here," Director Verde's voice says from behind me as she walks into the room. She's in workout attire herself, a strange sight compared to her usual garb. As if this is her typical routine, she joins me.

After she finishes a round of reps, I share with her, "I'm going to marry him."

"I assumed you would," she replies, unbothered by the news. "I gave him my blessing before he left here yesterday."

I hesitate before I tell her, "We're getting married in two weeks. Technically, two weeks from yesterday."

"That's probably smart," she agrees. "If you ripped up that forged certificate like I think you did, the sooner you marry him, the better for all of us. There's no point in putting it off for months from now when you've already made your decision to spend your life with him."

"Thank you for allowing us to make the choice," I say to the only blood family member of mine that I know. "And for ensuring that in becoming a princess, I'm not weak or defenseless walking into this."

"I promised your parents that I would take care of you, but you're old enough to take care of yourself now. They would be proud of the woman you've become. I have some things I'd like to give to you after we're done in here." It will still be another hour or so before Maria wakes up and finds my bed abandoned, so I take advantage of the calm before the storm of wedding details.

Forty-five minutes later, I follow Zeta through the halls where others are beginning to stir for the day. My comrades are silent as we pass them, either due to their respect for Director Verde or the news of my title change has already spread through the ranks. She leads me into her office and locks the door behind us. Behind her desk, she removes a few floorboards, revealing a chest hidden in the floor. I help her pull it out. Zeta unlocks it with a key she wears on a chain around her neck. On top of her hidden treasures is a pile of white tulle and lace. Zeta lifts it out of the chest, the fabric unfolding into a princess cut wedding gown with three-quarter sleeves.

"This was your mother's dress," she tells me as she holds it up for me to see. "Two weeks doesn't give much time to find and tailor a new dress, but if you want to wear this one, I think we can have it ready in time." Zeta hands me the fabric, and I hold it up against myself, picturing myself wearing it on my wedding day.

"It's perfect," I smile as I admire the detailed lace embroidery and silk buttons on the back.

Zeta says, "I'll have someone deliver it to Costella's when she opens. If you stop by her shop after lunch, she can get your measurements and start on any alterations."

"Thank you," I say to her for the second time today. "Having a dress is one less pressing detail to figure out today. Finding a venue is going to be a nightmare."

My older cousin shoots me a puzzled expression. She asks, "Lina, do you honestly think that any of the suitable places in Venezia are going to pass up the opportunity to host the wedding of the Crown Prince of Lazio and Duchess of Sozzini? Take Niccolò with you when you tour these places, and if they don't take his word on who he is, tell them to call me for verification. I'll set the record straight."

WHEN I WALK BACK into the house, the volume of noise in the kitchen clues me in to the presence of guests. Dario and Nic are with Maria and her mother, helping them set out breakfast and coffee. Nic is the first to notice my presence in the room as he walks over to pull me into a hug.

"I'm all gross and sweaty from working out," I complain to him as he refuses to let me go.

"I'm glad I didn't have to try to hunt you down to start wedding planning," Maria says, the relief evident in her tone.

Dario quips, "You mean you're glad you didn't have to send me to hunt her down?"

"Same thing," Maria smiles at him.

Trying again, I say to Nic as much as to everyone else, "In all seriousness, I need to go freshen up before diving into wedding stuff." While the others return their attention to breakfast, Nic follows me to my room for a moment of privacy. Careful not to close the door all the way when he walks in behind me, his lips meet mine, kissing me as if it were as instinctual as breathing. Standing in my bedroom alone with my fiancé, all I want to do is forget all our boundaries. I want to show him how much I love him, to be as close to him as physically possible. Any potentially conceived child would be legitimate to the throne in only thirteen days.

"We need to wait until after the wedding," he whispers, reading my thoughts and desires. "There's too much we have to plan and prepare in the next thirteen days, and when I make love to you, I want to do so as your husband. I also don't want to have to rush or worry about Dario or your family potentially walking in on us. I don't know if you've noticed, but your bedroom door doesn't have a lock on it."

I pout as I say, "You say that as if we'll have time for a honeymoon. Don't you have responsibilities waiting for you at the castle?"

"A large part of my responsibilities as heir apparent is to marry and produce my heir, which is precisely why a honeymoon is necessary. I'm taking care of the details for that, though, so all you need to do is pack and show up," he replies.

After a soft knock, Dario peeks his head into the room. With one eyebrow raised, he says, "Nic, your presence is requested in the kitchen. You know, I was bracing myself for what I might be walking in on, but I'm pleasantly surprised to find the door cracked open, and no clothing has been removed. You both get a passing grade for self-control."

"Yes, well, his Royal Highness is an honorable man who insists on waiting until the wedding night," I retort as I grab fresh clothes and push past both men to change in my bathroom. Behind me, I hear Nic's laugh and picture him shaking his head.

In the privacy of my bathroom, I allow myself to feel the relief that he wants to wait—relief that in thirteen days, we'll be alone in a hotel room as husband and wife without interruptions. As much as I'm looking forward to a honeymoon, I'm still nervous about it. Neither of us has any previous experience, which is both comforting and intimidating. He's right, though; we'll need to take our time to figure it out together, which would be impossible in my childhood bedroom or the twin bed in Dario's spare bedroom.

When I rejoin the group in the kitchen, they've already seated with coffee and food, leaving an open spot for me between Nic and Maria. A hot cappuccino awaits me, and I take my seat at the table. Nic's hand finds mine underneath the table as he interlaces our fingers.

"Did you see Director Verde this morning?" Dario asks me, his plate already scraped clean. My mother, Anna, gets up from her chair to spoon more food onto his plate. She adds more to Nic's plate as well, insisting that he needs it for the long day ahead.

"Yes, I didn't realize she has a habit of training before everyone else gets there," I say. "After we finished, we went to her office so she could give me my mother's wedding dress from storage. I'm supposed to go to Costella's this afternoon for measurements so she can have it ready for the wedding."

"She would have loved to see you wearing her dress," Anna beams. "I'll meet you and Maria at Costella's around two this afternoon. That should give you enough time to tour a few venues while I take care of the catering for the reception. Niccolò, don't forget to give me a list of your favorite dishes and wines before you leave. Lina, I'll make sure your green dress is clean and ready for the rehearsal dinner. Dario, are you training today, or are you looking at venues with the other three?"

Dario, whose plate is once again empty, leans back in the chair and replies, "I've been told my presence is required due to my responsibilities both as Nic's best man and as a future groom." It does make sense for Dario and Maria to tour the venues at the same time as us, given their recent engagement.

I turn to Nic in surprise, "You asked a guy you've known less than a week to be your best man? What about poor Franco?"

"Franco told me he's too busy with his new promotion to be my best man, and Dario is like a brother to you. Anyone who's your family is soon to be my family too," he explains.

Dario adds, "And it makes more sense since he's staying at my place until the wedding anyway. Someone has to tell him all your secrets before he's stuck with you for the rest of your lives."

IN MY ABSENCE the last few weeks, Maria had compiled a list of wedding venues she was considering, making it easier for me, given the short timeline. She and I have attended enough weddings to know which locations left much to be desired and which ones would make the wishlist. Though we share the same top five options, we rank them differently, mostly because, before recent events, I had a hard time picturing my wedding. Parts of my mind are still playing catch-up to the turn of events.

Nic's hand rests on my lower back as we walk through the tangle of Venetian streets. Some residents stare or take a second glance at him, and I know it's only a short time before word of the stranger spreads. By tomorrow, half the city will have learned about the wedding—about the crown prince marrying one of their own.

"How large a space do you think we'll need?" Nic asks me as we approach the first venue. "The guest list will all be people who come for you."

I pause a moment at the obvious statement. His only immediate family still alive is his father, the very reason my parents aren't here either. Despite being an orphan, I have family and friends here, and everyone he knows here is someone he knows because of me. I squeeze his hand and meet his eyes, "I'm coming for you."

"Do you think Director Verde intends to invite all the Resistance agents?" Maria asks both me and Dario, her eyes wide as her brain calculates those numbers.

The possibility doesn't faze Dario. "Just find a venue that you like and has the date available. We can make whatever adjustments are needed to fit what we have to work with."

In Maria's words, "Bauer Palazzo is the best place to check first, given their multiple terrace options, all of which boast stunning views." As we walk through the front doors, I remind myself that the ballroom at the castle where I first met Nic is much more grandiose than any other venue in the country. In another life, my wedding would take place in a castle and be attended by dignitaries and noble families; this tier of luxury is a step down compared to what my mother imagined for me.

At our arrival, the concierge observes our group of four. "Buongiorno! How can I help you?"

Maria takes the lead. "Buongiorno. I called about an hour ago to make an appointment to tour the wedding venues. It's for both me and my sister." Had she called all five places this morning to book these tours without my notice?

The concierge smiles in recognition. "Yes, I'll be the one showing you our options. My name is Daniella, and I'm the head of the wedding team at Bauer Palazzo. You two are Maria and Adelina, correct?" She and I both nod in confirmation.

"I'm Dario, Maria's fiancé," he introduces.

"I'm Nic, Adelina's fiancé," the prince says, the sound of the word bringing a smile to my lips. *Fiancé*. Daniella's gaze lingers on Nic for a few seconds longer than it had on Dario, but then she resumes her introduction.

"We'll start on the bottom and work our way up," she explains, and we follow her lead. The first terrace, De Pisis Terrace, overlooks the Canal Grando and accommodates seventy to eighty guests. It's beautiful and close to the water, but I'm keeping an open mind. I don't want to feel like I'm settling if this is the only available option. The restaurant of the same name shares the views through the windows. In a city as beautiful as this, it seems a waste to get married inside when the weather is cooperative.

The Grand Ballroom is larger, allowing for more guests, but it's too reminiscent of the ballroom where I once pretended the king's stare was of no consequence. Maria falls in love when she sees the Bar Canal Terrace. Though he tries to hide it, I suspect Dario shares Maria's excitement over the space and the view of the Canal Grando. Despite my fast-approaching wedding, I'm here to help her choose a venue as much as I'm here to find one of my own. Hours from now, I'll have to remind her of the ones that made her face light up like this spot.

Daniella certainly saves the most breathtaking view for the end. When I step out onto the Settimo Cielo Terrace, I feel sparks the same way I felt them when I saw Niccolò for the first time. The panorama around us serves as a bittersweet reminder that my future isn't in this city that I've called home for as long as I can remember. But the man who has become my new home is looking at this rooftop with an expression that mirrors my desires.

"This is the highest terrace in the city," Daniella recites to us as we walk around, my imagination fast-forwarding thirteen days from now in what might be an impossible dream. I'm so lost in my battle between elation and cynicism that I almost miss when Daniella tells us, "There was a cancellation, and this space is available for the day, thirteen days from now." Either she's telling the truth or someone told her who Nic is, making us a higher priority than whatever was originally planned on that date. There's no sure way to know the truth, so I push the thought away.

Nic sees the way my face lights up and says, "Yes, absolutely, we'll take it."

Zeta does more than send the dress to Costella's; she's with Anna, waiting for me and Maria when we arrive at the shop. Costella herself is inspecting my mother's wedding dress, which is currently being worn by a mannequin. Dario and Nic are looking at suits on their own in another shop a few streets away.

"How did the venue tours go?" Anna asks us as she embraces her daughter.

We still went to the other locations on Maria's list, but ultimately, the Bar Canal Terrace was voted the favorite by both Maria and Dario. Before coming to Costella's, we made a second stop at Bauer Palazzo so they could choose a wedding date a few months from now.

"Both weddings are at Bauer Palazzo," I say loud enough for Zeta to hear. "Thirteen days from now at Settimo Cielo Terrace." I stay quiet about any suspicions regarding Zeta or someone else pulling strings to make that happen.

Noting my presence, Costella removes the dress from the mannequin and shoves it in my arms with orders for me to undress and for Maria to help me put on the wedding dress. Costella is more than talk, though, because she assists Maria with the buttons on the back of the bodice. Seeing my reflection in the mirror, my olive suntanned skin glowing against the delicate white lace, is what makes this finally feel real. At Costella's guidance, I walk out of the dressing area to show Anna and Zeta. There's a collective approval among the women as Zeta adds a tiara to my head as a finishing touch.

"Lina, you look like a princess," Maria says with admiration. Another glance at my reflection confirms her statement. I can already picture the expression on Niccolò's face when he sees me on our wedding day, looking like his princess.

CHAPTER 14

Niccolò

Either my updated status as Lina's fiancé has granted me clearance, or Dario was playing a prank on me the first time, because when I accompany him to the Resistance base for my second visit, the blindfold isn't even mentioned. Just like Lina, Dario is so accustomed to his routine and training schedule that skipping more than one day at the gym makes him restless. With the most significant details of the wedding now decided—the venue, the food, our attire—he insists that we can at least spend our mornings in the training rooms. My curiosity far outweighs any misgivings I have about joining him.

When we walk into the main area, Lina is in the designated kickboxing zone sparring with Franco. Her laser focus doesn't register my presence, allowing me to observe her in her element. Her jabs are fast and precise, and my heart swells with pride at the sight.

"Not exactly how you imagined your future princess," Dario whispers in my ear, his tone amused.

I reply quietly, "Joke's on you; I happen to be very attracted to the idea of a princess who can beat me up. Can't forget that she almost killed me on the night that we met." I beam at the realization of how far we've come since then.

Franco is the first to notice our presence, and he holds up his hands in surrender to signal his need for a break. She follows his gaze and turns around to see us. When her eyes meet mine, her entire being visibly lights up. For a moment, I forget that we're not the only ones in the training room. She pulls off her gloves before walking over to me. Despite the layer of sweat across her skin, my arms are outstretched to pull her into a hug. I overhear Franco say to Dario, "Imagine being around them when they were trying to deny their feelings for each other. The awkward tension was almost unbearable."

Dario, Franco, and Lina take me through a condensed version of their typical training day. I push to keep up with the three agents, grateful for the sessions I'd had with Franco and Lina at the various safe houses. I can feel the eyes of the other agents on me as they observe the crown prince on their territory, hanging out with the elite within their ranks.

After a few hours, Director Verde comes by to join the onlookers. After a few minutes, she calls, "Nic and Lina, let's go meet in my office." She and I towel off and refill our water bottles before following Zeta through the maze of hallways. My hand finds Lina's as our fingers intertwine. From the corner of my eye, I can see her satisfied smile. As much as I want to stop and taste that smile, I resist the urge. The mood today is a stark difference compared to that of my first visit to this office.

"I hope it's okay that Dario let me tag along," I start when we've all taken our seats.

"Nic, I'm glad you've taken an interest," Zeta replies with a smile. "That's why I wanted to talk to you two today. The other day, when you asked about my family—our family—I omitted information about the present condition of the

Sozzini estate. While there was evidence that your father tried to track down Alessandro, Valentina, and Lina, most of what remained was untouched. Once I was certain that he had given up on searching there again, I tasked a regiment of Resistance agents to maintain the estate and increase security. It's now the location of the other Resistance base."

"Wait," Lina says on the edge of her seat in understanding and excitement, "the base in Siena is on our family estate?" This is the first time I've heard mention of a second base. In what little he let slip about the Resistance, my father never mentioned more than one possible base, either, which means he likely doesn't know. Even Lina and Franco had been mute about the other location.

Zeta continues, "It's technically your rightful inheritance, Lina. I don't know if the two of you have discussed what happens after the wedding regarding where you'll reside and how to keep Lina safe from the king, but I wanted to present you with this option before you make a decision. It's well-guarded, and it would give you time. If you choose to go to Siena, you'll be in charge of the base." Whether Lina has put the pieces together yet or not, I understand the meaning behind Zeta's words. Had Lina either killed me or chosen not to be with me, she would still be given this option because she's earned it. The roundabout route back to Venezia was as much about safety as it was about exposing her to other parts of the country, making her world bigger.

Lina looks at me for clarity, the possibilities churning through her head. She's processing the news, but she wants my opinion on the matter. This is a decision we must make together.

"Lina, I would follow you anywhere as long as I know you'll be safe," I simply say to my future wife. "I proposed to you, intending to build a life together, wherever that is. I don't need to live in the castle while my father is alive, and I'm done with him trying to control my life. If Siena is as safe as you say, then that's where we'll live."

Director Verde shares more details about the exact location of the estate as well as the top agents who are running the base. The main house has been relatively empty except for when Zeta visits the property. The more she discloses, the more I suspect that my father might be aware of its existence; however, knowing its location doesn't mean he can penetrate the security that now surrounds it. He likely knows that if he attacks Siena, he'll be starting a war he's unsure he can win.

Dario's apartment is full of sound and energy with Maria, Lina, and Franco joining Dario and me for a Chef Nic dinner specialty. When Franco had spilled the beans about how much I had cooked during our multi-city trek, Dario insisted that we all should experience my skills together. Lina volunteered to accompany me to the grocery store as a way to craft some alone time with me. The moment our friends had veered off in another direction, she pulled me close for a kiss that almost made me forget what we were supposed to be doing.

Having helped me with all the prepping, Lina stays by my side in the kitchen, stealing glances and kisses while we watch and stir the polenta. One day, when I'm king, taking the time to cook a meal will be a rare luxury, but for now, I bask in this peaceful moment before my wedding. My fiancée wears a contented smile as she observes me at the stove and her lifelong friends sitting at the dining room table.

"Are you sure that you want to take over the Siena base?" I ask her quietly so the others don't overhear. "I can't promise we would be safe here in Venezia long-term. I would have to go back to the villa and pick up my car and then grab some of my belongings from the castle, but I'm sure there's a way I can do all that without leaving a trail back here. I don't know how often I can make that trip covertly, though."

I watch her chest rise and fall as she breathes deeply before responding. "Nic, Venezia is an island, which is both good and bad in terms of safety. As much as I would love to spend my whole life here with the people I've grown up with, our staying here long-term might endanger them. I want to spend some time in the place where I should have grown up with my parents. With different circumstances, Siena would have been a big part of our childhood, I'm sure. I can't shake the feeling that there might be answers there too—answers about my parents and why my family became a target."

"I agree," I say without hesitation, stirring the hot porridge before meeting her gaze again. "Without an assassination mission to aim for, it doesn't make sense for you to stay here without anything to challenge you. I know your training schedule has become routine for you, but we're getting married. Everything is about to change for both of us, either way."

"How are we going to get away from the castle once we go back?" It's a question I anticipate from her because it's something I mull over between all the wedding planning.

I also don't miss what she's said, knowing her well enough by now. "You're not coming with me. It's not up for debate." My declaration comes out louder than I intended, catching the attention of the three in the room next to us.

"Assuming Nic is referring to the castle," Dario cuts in, his statement directed at Lina, "he's right. It was one thing to sneak in on a night that the castle was full of guests, but it's another entirely to go at a time when anyone might notice you. The more I think about it, we're all fortunate that the king didn't recognize you at the ball, considering he knew your parents. I'd be surprised if you don't look a lot like one or both of them."

"A princess who can't even enter her own castle," Lina retorts with an eye roll.

Amused, I remind her, "Sweetheart, it's not your castle. It's not even my castle yet if you want to be technical. Siena is yours, though, since marrying me doesn't require rescinding your rights."

Dario and I have already discussed the post-honeymoon logistics, and I nod to him to share our plans with Lina now. "When your honeymoon is over, Maria and I are going to drive you and Nic down to the villa in Napoli to pick up his car. Then, he's going to the castle while the three of us drive to Siena. Once Nic has finished what he needs to do at the castle, he's going to join us as quickly and as safely as he can in Siena. Maria and I will stay with you until he arrives."

Lina's eyes turn to mine, searching. She looks as if she wants to argue every possible vantage point and flaw to the plan, but she resists because she knows Dario and I have already gone through all she would bring up. Defeated, she says to us, "I guess that could work. Plus, I don't hate the idea of having Dario and Maria around to help me get acquainted with the estate. It'll be nice to have some extra time with them."

"I love the idea of seeing other parts of the country!" Maria exclaims, clearly having heard the news at the same time as Lina. Dario might be a man in love, but he knows when to keep his mouth shut until the right time. It put me at ease knowing I can trust him.

"Man, way to make a guy feel left out," Franco jokes before adding, "but I already have plans anyway. I have a lot of training to do if I'm going to run a new base. I suspected we were sent to specific checkpoints for that reason, and I'm glad that Ancona makes the most sense for both my next step and for the Resistance's next expansion. Long-distance relationships are never a permanent solution; someone either moves or the relationship ends."

The news of a third base, merely a few hours after hearing about the second, makes one thing very clear: the Resistance is preparing for a possible civil war against my father's rule. Against my father, not against me or the monarchy or nobility. Seeing the way they've welcomed me with open arms and given Director Verde's invitation for Lina and me to live together in Siena, these moves are in preparation for a strong defense if my father were the one to incite an attack. Another glance at Lina and the way her engagement ring reflects in the light confirms another suspicion—when my father learns of my marriage to Lina, it may become the catalyst for such violence. Until an heir is conceived or even born, I certainly won't be the one to tell him the news. Even then, Lina may not be safe from the king. After all that, they might both still be in danger.

"Hey, are you okay?" Lina asks, noticing my somber mood. I shake my head to communicate a response while attempting to return my thoughts to the present. She lightly kisses my cheek and holds my hand that isn't stirring the polenta. "If I had killed you with an arrow, this country would already be at war. It's a real possibility that all of us here have been at least mentally prepared for. I know it can't be easy being at odds with your only living family when the stakes are this high."

"Lina," I say, pulling the polenta off the stovetop and fixing my entire attention on her. "You are my family now. You're the one I'm making vows to in less than two weeks. If loving and protecting you means I'm at war with my father, then come what may."

Franco walks towards us to move the pan of polenta with the rest of the dinner dishes. "If you two are finished discussing our possible future deaths or monarchy takeovers, I've been waiting hours for this food."

DARIO and I review the wedding checklist while drinking our coffees, the sunrise fading from early vibrancy into the pastel colors that invade the sky before the blue of daytime. The honeymoon reservation, rehearsal dinner location, and menu still need to be verified today. With all of us focusing our energy on this task, planning a wedding in a fortnight has become less daunting. We are finally solidifying the other events surrounding the momentous occasion.

"When you left the castle, did it cross your mind that you might marry before returning?" Dario asks me.

I think back to those hours of painstaking planning and waiting for my birthday extravaganza. "I knew that, assuming my return to the castle was voluntary, there could only be one of two outcomes: either my betrothed had died or I would find her alive. With how legally binding the betrothal is, I assumed that finding her would result in marrying her, even if she had been a stranger. But it's different imagining it than planning the wedding. Seeing her face and knowing her name—finding out that it's been Adelina this whole time made more sense than anything in my life has for a very long time."

"I should have warned you sooner," Dario begins, taking a sip of cappuccino before continuing, "but apart from the obvious state secrets, anything you tell me can and might be used in my best man speech."

"And that is why I'm glad I asked you to be the best man instead of Franco," I joke. "Imagine all the inappropriate references he might make in a reception speech."

"Instead, I'll make some black widow jokes," Dario teases. "I wish I could have been a fly on the wall when Lina had her arrow aimed at you, and you convinced her not to release it."

I shake my head while the memory washes over me. "She hadn't even told me her real name. I hope she used the fake name the entire time at the ball because my father might have heard her real first name at some point decades ago. The less he knows, the better."

"She did," Dario assures me. "It was one of those details we went over before she left. I called her by that fake name for a few days leading up to her departure from Venezia. Her training was thorough. In the face of possible war, I'm more worried about you than her."

Stunned by his confession, I make one of my own. "I haven't said anything because it hasn't come up, but I feel the need to remind you that I'm the crown prince. I didn't spend years out of the public eye inside a castle, reading books and learning laws the entire time. My father was relentless when it came to preparing me to be king one day, and that included countless lessons in archery, swordplay, and many of the other areas you and Lina focused on. I didn't train six days a week at the same intensity, but I did train with some of the best teachers in the country. I can go up against you or Lina right now in archery, and I guarantee it will be a close match." I'm not trying to sound arrogant or overconfident; I'm merely tired of being underestimated among a group of elite agents.

Two hours later, Dario and I are at the Resistance-owned archery range, with Lina and Maria watching, cheering, and judging our head-to-head battle. The winner of this round goes up against Lina in the next, sparking my inner competitiveness. The feeling reminds me of my childhood when I would compete with my brother, always wanting to prove myself; I've missed the challenge and adrenaline.

At the end of the third set, Dario concedes, telling Lina, "He's better than I was expecting, but you can beat him." Right now, it's the closest to a compliment he's willing to give me after his close loss to me.

Though one of us could easily be a distraction to the other, we respect each other's concentration space. We're equally in the zone and evenly matched, the third set resulting in a tie. To break the tie, we each shoot one last arrow, Lina being the first. I release a breath when the arrow leaves my bow, and I finally fix my eyes on my competitor. She's already watching me in admiration. I silently pray she always looks at me like that. Hand in hand, we walk toward the target where Dario is inspecting the tiebreaker. Unable to trust his eyes, Dario retrieves a tape measure to determine whose arrow is closer to the center.

Seeing the measurements, Lina pulls me in for a short kiss and says, "I'm glad we're on the same side." Beating Lina feels as if I've passed an unknown test.

CHAPTER 15

Adelina

As promised, my green dress is ready for the rehearsal dinner the day before the wedding. I've only worn it once before to a wedding, given my typical wardrobe before the ball consisted of clothing suitable for physical training.

"This is the last night we'll be sharing a bedroom," Maria's voice says from our bathroom. "I mean, I knew this day was coming due to my engagement, but I didn't think I would have to say goodbye to you again so soon." Her voice drifts closer as she joins me in the bedroom. In all the wedding planning, I hadn't even finished unpacking from my month of traveling with Franco and Nic, and now nearly all my belongings were sitting in bags and suitcases. Most would stay here until the end of the honeymoon, but Maria had helped me pack the one meant for the honeymoon with new clothes.

"It's certainly not the new beginning I would have pictured the last time I was leaving," I reply with a laugh. "The prince wasn't the only one left defenseless."

Maria pulls me into a hug. "I've never been so happy to be right. Now, we have a rehearsal dinner to get through before we marry you off to your betrothed. At least we know your parents would have approved." She would know how to bring out the humor in the whole thing.

I had no involvement in planning the rehearsal dinner, the responsibility being Dario's and Nic's, with help from Anna. It's the kick-off to a whirlwind twenty-four hours that ends with a honeymoon. I fuss with the straps of the dress to keep my hands busy. The ruby pendant from Nic hangs around my neck nearly every day when I'm not dressed in exercise attire.

Anna peeks her head in the door. "I'm here for final inspections before we leave." The rest of her body emerges, donned in a black A-line dress. Since my traditional dress for the rehearsal is green, the rest of the guests were encouraged to wear neutral colors to avoid any clashing. While I would credit Anna for that idea, it could have just as well been my groom.

There's an abundance of wine for our intimate group as the courses of food are eaten in earnest. As expected, Dario stands to give a brief toast before the pasta course.

"I'll keep this one short since I have another speech at the reception dinner tomorrow," Dario says with a wink that would have made half the women in Venezia swoon had they been in attendance. "Even though I'm the best man, the bride is practically family to me. I wasn't sure what kind of man would be good enough for Lina when she was finally ready to open her heart to someone, but the more time I spend with Prince Niccolò, the more convinced I am that he might be the only one who could have possibly been her best match. Per cent'anni."

I can feel the threat of tears at Dario's heartfelt words, but I raise my glass of wine and take another sip of the Prosecco I opted for, the fizz dancing across my tongue before I swallow. Soon, the buzz from the toast dies down again as mouths are filled with homemade pasta. When our hands aren't holding utensils or wineglasses, Nic and I touch under the table, dancing fingertips across palms and the soft skin of wrists. The butterflies in my stomach are just as lively as they were when we met. In our only private moment, his goodnight kiss leaves me devastated when he pulls away.

"I don't want to say goodnight," I say into his shoulder, shying away from the intensity of his gaze.

"The next time I kiss you, we'll be husband and wife," he replies, his lips brushing my ear. "Tomorrow, we won't have to say goodbye to each other. Tomorrow night, we don't even have to sleep if you don't want to." I hit him lightly and roll my eyes.

"This is how it should be," I say with a satisfied sigh. "I hope we always feel like this—like we can never get enough of each other."

THE MORNING DRAGS ON, the seconds somehow slowing. At Maria's instruction, Dario forbade me from going to the base to do any training, citing the "potential for injury and bruising" as the reason. As much as I hate to skip today, knowing I won't be going during my honeymoon, I know they're right. To train at the base is to invite the risk of something swelling later, no matter how careful I am. The activity in the house starts around sunrise, but I pretend to sleep until I know breakfast is nearly ready.

"You can stop pretending now," Maria says to me as she shuffles through every bag of makeup she owns.

With the reception at Bauer Palazzo, our living room serves as the designated hair and makeup station for our preparations. The Basilica di San Marco is only a seven-minute walk away from Bauer Palazzo, but it's through a very public space. If word has traveled the way I assume it has, crowds will be gathered in the piazza following the ceremony. The people of my city will come to see their crown prince and his bride. The seven-minute walk could take an hour in the worst-case scenario. I know the start times of the ceremony and reception, but the details are in Maria's hands.

I follow her into the kitchen, the smells of my favorites mingling in the air. "Good morning," I say to my family, holding back the bittersweet wave trying to overtake my emotions. This is worse than the morning I left for the ball, despite it being the happiest occasion I could have wished for.

Over breakfast, Maria recites the checklists and schedules, more to remind our parents than for us. This is easy memorization compared to navigating the castle corridors. Besides, being the bride means nothing starts without me anyway.

"Lina, are you even listening to me?" Maria asks, the annoyance evident in her tone. Once she's certain she's recaptured my attention, she says, "I was reminding you to make sure you have your honeymoon luggage ready. Dario is coming by in an hour to pick it up and drop it off at Bauer Palazzo, so you have it with you when you leave the reception later. Unless you have plans to go naked the whole time, make sure your clothes are packed."

Despite her worries that something will go forgotten, this is not it. I packed the honeymoon bag a few nights ago when my thoughts were louder than my need to sleep. Though Nic refuses to give me any details about said honeymoon, it's safe enough to guess that it's going to be on one of the many islands in the lagoon. Climate and weather are fairly consistent this time of year.

As expected, Dario is punctual in arriving an hour later. With my luggage in hand, he's almost out the front door when he says, "Oh, wait, Lina, Nic wanted me to pass along the message that he's written his vows, but he doesn't expect you to do the same."

The prince has done what now? I'm temporarily frozen at the news. This was not a detail either of us had brought up at any point. "I have to write my vows if he's doing so. It's only fair," I say as my mouth rises to the challenge before my brain has fully processed this last-minute task.

"Hey, I'm just the messenger," Dario says with his hands in the air to emphasize his innocence.

Having overheard, Maria tells her fiancé, "Dario, go take care of the luggage. Lina, write. You don't have much time before we have to start hair and makeup. I knew there would be something."

I obey her directive without any argument, rushing to my room. A few minutes later, the blank page mocks me for my inability to verbalize the depth of my love for my soon-to-be husband. Maria knocks on the door as a warning before she slips in.

"Writer's block?" She's calmed down since Dario's announcement. I nod in response to her question. "Lina, why did you say yes when he asked you to marry him?"

I reflect on that whirlwind day two weeks ago, full of life-altering truths and paths. "I can't imagine a future without him. If I had to choose all of him or none of him, I'm all in every time."

Maria smiles and says, "Write that down. See, it's not as hard as you're making it. Just write all the reasons you're excited for the rest of your life with him. I'll make sure we all use the waterproof mascara."

She leaves me to finish my task, and the words flow easily.

THE GIRL'S reflection in the red dress at the ball was sultry and alluring in a nearly regal way, commanding attention. Though the same girl now wears a white dress, she appears softer in a way that brings out her beauty, yet she seems effortlessly regal. The tiara pinned to my head solidifies the princess persona. Seeing myself like this makes it impossible to ignore how much I look the part of a prince's bride.

"You look like your mother did on her wedding day," Zeta says, and the statement lifts my heart in a way words can't capture. I made the unorthodox decision to ask both Zeta and my father to walk me down the aisle, a symbol of both blood bonds and chosen family, presenting me on my wedding day.

"Don't you have a groom to attend to?" Maria asks Dario as he saunters into the small chamber.

"He's fine," Dario shrugs. "Just pacing a little and reading the vows he wrote. I wanted to see my protégé."

I roll my eyes and turn around to show off the wedding dress. Dario's eyes soften as he takes in my appearance. "Don't go soft on me now, Dario. You didn't cry when you were sending me off on an assassination attempt."

"Nic is going to be a mess when he sees you," Dario says. "You're getting married, Lina."

The last fifteen minutes before the start of the ceremony fly by in a blur. Dario leaves us to return to his duty as best man. I quickly scan the paper where I wrote my vows, reminding myself of the words before my speech. I can hear the music through the door as I stand with Zeta to my left and my father on the right. On cue, the doors swing open, revealing the room full of guests—a large percentage of Resistance agents—standing and waiting. My eyes search for my anchor with the priest at the other end of the aisle. My heart races at the sight of Prince Niccolò in a gray tuxedo, his expression fighting back tears. If I didn't have anyone accompanying me, I would have rushed to close the gap between us. When I've been given away, he takes my hands in his with a tight squeeze of assurance.

"You look beautiful," he mouths to me.

The priest asks us, "Niccolò Mattei and Adelina Sozzini, have you come here to enter into marriage without coercion, freely and wholeheartedly?"

"I have," we say in unison.

The priest follows up with the second traditional question. "Are you prepared, as you follow the path of marriage, to love and honor each other for as long as you both shall live?"

"I am," our voices blend in response.

"Are you prepared to accept children lovingly from God and to bring them up according to the law of Christ and his Church?"

In response to the third question, we once again confirm, "I am."

In the exchange of consent, the priest addresses me to repeat after him. "I, Duchess Adelina Pace Sozzini of the House of Sozzini, take you, Prince Niccolò Alessandro Mattei of the House of Mattei, to be my husband. I promise to be true to you in good times and in bad, in sickness and in health. I will love you and honor you all the days of my life."

Next, Nic does the same. "I, Prince Niccolò Alessandro Mattei of the House of Mattei, take you, Duchess Adelina Pace Sozzini of the House of Sozzini, to be my wife. I promise to be true to you in good times and in bad, in sickness and in health. I will love you and honor you all the days of my life."

After the exchange of rings and the vows that accompany, the priest informs our guests that we have decided to exchange our written vows in addition to the traditional ones. This time, Nic volunteers to go first.

"Adelina, I knew from the first moment that I laid eyes on you that you were someone I would never be able to forget," he says, looking at me as if we were the only ones in the room. "I felt as if I'd been struck by lightning, forever changed simply because I had gotten a few small moments with you. I never would have imagined I would have the privilege of being here with you today, and not just because you almost killed me later that night. For weeks, I thought the betrothal would be the thing that would tear us apart, but I'll be eternally grateful that in the end, it's always been you. It seems too good to be true that I get to choose you. For the rest of my life, it will be you every day. I vow always to choose you and love you."

I breathe deeply, hoping it will hold back the dam of emotions and tears threatening to release at his words. Though I have my own words written down to read from, seeing his blue eyes now ensures me that I don't need them.

From the heart, I recite, "Niccolò—Nic—a large part of my life has revolved around you. For years, I trained with one mission and goal in mind, thinking that my sole purpose was to end your life. I knew that once it was over, my life wouldn't be the same. I was right that it would change my life, but not in the way I'd always assumed. I guess it's only fitting that I would fall hopelessly in love with the prince I had been obsessed with for most of my life. That mission was a lost cause from the moment you helped me off the ballroom floor and asked me to dance with you. Finding you helped me find a piece of myself, the parts of my history that had been hidden away. I love you and choose our future together. I choose to build a family and a kingdom with you, whatever may come. It's you and me in this together because I can't imagine my life without you in it."

Together with our guests, we partake in mass. We go through the traditions of the nuptial blessing and sign the marriage certificate. The space between Nic and me buzzes with anticipation after seeing our names etched on the official document. I almost miss when the priest announces our new titles as Prince and Princess, husband and wife, to the guests. I don't miss the moment when Nic's lips are on mine before the priest can finish his statement to kiss the bride. He leaves me breathless and dizzy for what won't be the last time today. Dario hands us the glass vase to break, and our combined strength shatters the vase into an uncountable number of fragments, enough to signify a lifetime together. We linger behind to take a few photos in the chapel with my family and Dario while the guests begin the walk to the reception.

"How does it feel to be a princess?" Nic whispers in my ear, his lips brushing the hyper-sensitive skin as the photographer captures the moment.

I wrack my brain for a clever response before I settle on, "I don't think it will feel real until I order some people around."

"You can order me around," he offers, his meaning clear by his sultry tone.

"We still have a reception to get through," I remind him, both grateful and impatient at the buffer of time separating us from the wedding night.

Once the photographer is satisfied with his photos at the chapel, Dario and Maria join us again. As best man and maid of honor, they ensured that the belongings we brought to the chapel are now at the Bauer Palazzo with our luggage. When we walk out the front doors of the Basilica into the piazza, the crowds swarm with excitement. Nic's grip on my hand tightens as we hear our names echo across the groups of people gathered. A few steps in, the group throws rice as a symbol of fertility. Once the initial shock fades, we smile and greet those who personally congratulate us, and a few shopkeepers give us wedding gifts. Dario, acting in his role as both best man and Resistance agent, hovers near us as we slowly make our way across the piazza. If I didn't know better, I would think nearly the whole city had gathered in this space. Deep down, a part of me had been worried about how the people would react once word of Nic's identity spread, but seeing their welcoming of us is a relief I hadn't known I needed.

In the center of the piazza, Nic pauses, pulling me close to him. Before I can ask him what's going on, his free hand rests beneath my jaw, tilting my mouth to his in a kiss. Cheers erupt around us as I struggle to catch my breath. In all the planning, I hadn't mentally prepared myself for all the displays of public affection required during the wedding and reception. Despite his lack of public events within the past few years, my husband possesses the intuition to know how to win over his audience.

"They adore you almost as much as I do," he whispers in my ear.

"At least half of them are here to see you," I say as Dario ushers us again in the direction of Bauer Palazzo. Zeta and Anna are waiting for us in the lobby.

Daniella appears as if out of thin air with a clipboard in her hand and a headset. "Are you two ready to make your entrance at the reception, or do you want a few minutes to freshen up?"

Niccolò turns to me, gesturing for me to make the decision. As tempting as the prospect of a few minutes away from everyone seems, I don't trust myself in a room alone with him. My heart is too full for only a few minutes of solitude. "Let's make our entrance."

He never lets go of my hand as we climb the stairs together, but rather holds on as if I'm what's tethering him to the ground in this moment. It seems appropriate and ironic to feel as if I'm floating as we take each step higher to the Settimo Cielo Terrace. I hadn't noticed the sun inching downward on the horizon while we walked through the piazza, but as we stepped into the gathering of cheers and applause, I was swept away by the panoramic view of my favorite place at sunset. The visual is so perfect I nearly cry for the second time today.

"You with this backdrop might be the most stunning thing I will ever witness in my life," my husband says, reminding me of where and when we are. He leads me to the table set up for the two of us, Prosecco already bubbling in the glasses. Before I can even think about sitting down, he spins me into a dipping kiss, so smooth that I swoon despite the surprise of it. With how much we've already kissed and embraced today, my nerves about the wedding night give way to a hunger similar to what I'd felt that first night he kissed me. Now there are rings on our hands along with a legal document and vows binding us together for the rest of our lives.

The adrenaline must have been taming down my hunger because as soon as there's food in front of me, I notice how starving I am. Out of the corner of my eye, I catch Nic's amused expression as he watches me devour the ravioli. The differences in our upbringing are glaringly obvious. Despite the rumbling in his stomach that I could hear on repeat since we were posing for photos after the ceremony, he takes his time as he eats. If this were the first time sharing a meal with him, I would assume he's a slow eater; however, we've been together for more meals than not since the night we met. Nic is not a slow eater by any means. Nic is a prince who behaves with impeccable etiquette when the circumstance calls for it. Given that this is our wedding reception, I follow his lead for the next course.

"Despite any manners you may have witnessed from me before, I did have to learn basic etiquette to know how to blend in seamlessly at your ball," I say to him as I match his eating pace.

"I was thoroughly enjoying watching you eat," he says in a way that both melts me on the inside and makes me want to gently slap him for being cheesy. "Although I was concerned that at that pace, you might overeat and spend the remainder of the night with an upset stomach."

I say, "Good thing you made a vow that includes both sickness and health."

"Trust me, I was only thinking of you," he says, and I'm not sure how much of that is true. Yes, he is kind and considerate, but I can't imagine he's being entirely selfless. The skepticism must be evident on my face because he then admits, "It would also ruin any intentions to consummate this marriage tonight."

"Wow, so romantic," I say sarcastically with a smile. "Consummate."

"It's a safe word in a public space where anyone can overhear," he says in defense.

I lower my voice when I say, "I don't think anyone at this wedding reception has any misconceptions about what we'll be doing when we leave tonight. There was a point in history when bedding ceremonies were held to ensure the marriage couldn't be annulled."

"There are some traditions that are better left in the past," he says, the volume of his voice matching mine—loud enough to hear each other, but quiet enough to ensure no one can eavesdrop. With the music and conversation surrounding us, it's not hard to have a private conversation with him. "Fine, since you want romance on our wedding day, I'll rephrase that. I don't want you to overeat because when I finally get you alone for our first night as husband and wife, I want to be able to show you how much I love you. I've wanted to give you all of myself since the moment I met you, but I've been patiently waiting until tonight."

I fail to hide my blush from him. When my mind fails to come up with a worthy response, I say, "We still have dessert and dancing to get through before we can even think about leaving."

"I know," he says with a sigh. "And a boat ride to get to our honeymoon accommodations." It's the first hint he's given me about the next week, and it's not new information I hadn't already assumed. Most of the honeymoon destinations are on other islands in the lagoon.

"We could stay here tonight and save the boat ride for the morning," I suggest.

Nic shakes his head and says, "I don't trust myself to want to get out of bed in the morning. Planning a wedding in two weeks hasn't exactly been a relaxing task."

"In that case, we need espresso," I say as I spot the coffee being served with the dessert. When I stand up in hopes of catching the waiter's attention, a wave of clinking spreads like a ripple across the wedding guests. I feel the heat of Nic's body when he stands up next to me. It takes my brain a moment to remember that we're the bride and groom they're waiting to see kiss. His hands slip to my lower back as he pulls me close, forcing my gaze to his.

"Brace yourself," he says in warning before his lips silence my unspoken question. My brain hardly registers when he lifts me without breaking contact. Cheers and whistles erupt as he gently sets me down and distances himself enough to look at me. "I wanted to get creative. I wouldn't want you to get bored with kissing me so much today."

"Trust me, I could never get bored with you," I say while I will my racing heart to calm. "If anything, each one gets better than the last."

Maria walks over to us, holding a pair of scissors. "As nice as that tie is," she says as she points to Nic, "you know the rules. It's time to cut it up."

"But I don't need guests to contribute to the expenses," he argues. "I happen to be one of the wealthiest people in attendance. Plus, I'm sure Lina will have enough people willing to pay for a dance with her."

They turn to me to be the tiebreaker. "I like that tie too much to cut it up for a mere tradition," I say, taking Nic's side. "Can we start the toasts and dancing? We still have a boat to catch before the night is over."

Maria waves Dario over, and he quickly springs from his chair at her gesture as if he's been waiting for his cue. On his way over to us, he grabs a microphone and a glass of Prosecco. Satisfied with the progression of events, Nic and I return to our table.

THE FAIRY LIGHTS decorating the terrace twinkle like stars against the darkening dusk as Nic spins me in our first dance. The moment has both a sense of déjà vu and also feels entirely new, with colorful paper streamers tied to our hands. "I'm still wrapping my head around your admission that you've always been obsessed with me," he says in a whisper as we sway to the music.

I roll my eyes, but then I say, "I've been obsessed with you my whole life, even if most of that was planning your murder." I feel the low rumble of his chuckle more than I hear it. "But I'm glad I didn't kill you."

"If I were going to be assassinated by anyone, though, I would have wanted it to be you," he says and kisses my forehead. "And if you hadn't let me come with you, I would have exhausted everything to find you."

"To find me Lina or to find me the heiress to the Sozzini duchy?" I ask, knowing it's a complicated question.

He puts enough distance between us to lock his eyes with mine. "Both, I guess. I was already looking for my betrothed, but I would have had to add you to the list. It's surreal to think back to that night at the ball. Neither of us had any idea, and yet here we are. I don't remember everything my mother taught me about God and faith, but I'm convinced God has to be real for us to be here right now. It's too orchestrated to be accidental."

"You're probably right about that," I say in agreement. The song comes to an end before I can say more. The upbeat music welcomes our guests as they join the dance floor. When "La Tarantella" begins to play, no one can resist the traditional group dance as we hold hands in a circle and move clockwise. Song after song, we celebrate, surrounded by the village that raised an orphan girl in hiding from the king.

As we make our final rounds, the jolt of explosions fills the sky. Fireworks illuminate the night in bursts in the air and reflections off the water. As if the gathering in the Piasa San Marco earlier weren't enough, the whole city is commemorating the occasion now.

"It's been a long time since we've had something significant enough to warrant fireworks," Zeta says to us without any surprise in her tone.

"Somehow, I suspect those were originally intended as a

celebration for Lina's successful mission," Nic says jokingly, though I know there's truth to his statement.

"This is a greater success than that would have been," she reassures him.

The Bauer Palazzo's proximity to the water serves as an ideal docking place for the escape boat Niccolò prearranged to take us to our final destination for the night. Dario helps the captain load our luggage while Nic unnecessarily carries me on board. Unnecessary and charming are not mutually exclusive. With the firework smoke carried away in the breeze and the fairy lights of the terrace out of view, the moon and stars are easier to locate in the vast darkness above us.

"Have fun, but not too much fun?" Dario tells us more as a question than as a warning. "I guess the ideal outcome would be a honeymoon baby. Nic, make sure she takes an actual vacation. I'm not saying she can't do any exercise or training, but you only get one honeymoon. Lina, try not to kill the poor guy when he makes you try new things or asks you not to spend hours in the gym."

"I didn't marry her to try to control what she does," Nic says affectionately as his arm around my waist tightens. "But I can promise to keep her so busy and distracted with other things that training is the last thing on her mind."

Before Dario and I can unpack the intention behind my husband's words, the captain yells at us, the specific words drowned out by the sound of the boat's engine erupting to life. The ruckus renders it impossible to continue our goodbyes as the boat distances itself from the dock. Slowly, the lights of the city fade away, leaving only the moonlight to illuminate Nic's features.

"Guess what," he says into my ear so I can hear him above the engine's roar. He doesn't wait for my answer before he continues, "I'm now the handsome prince who both loves you and belongs with you forever. As future king and your husband, I'm removing all those boundaries we previously had since they're now irrelevant."

I search my mind for a clever response, but my thoughts short-circuit when he kisses my jawline rather than pulling away. He takes his time inching closer to my mouth, and rather than close my eyes to focus on the sensation, I gaze at the half moon's reflection in the dark lagoon waves. When his lips finally land on mine, though, he becomes the epicenter of my senses. Time stretches and shrinks as we thoroughly savor our first kiss of the day without an audience. It's familiar territory, nothing we haven't already explored, but I'm still not used to the way my heart races at his touch. For the minutes that I'm lost in him, I forget we're on a boat toward an unknown destination. I hardly notice as an island gradually grows closer as if it were moving nearer to us rather than the contrary.

From the moment the captain secures the boat to the dock at what appears to be a private entrance, concierges immediately appear to transport the luggage that Nic hands them. It's not until he's lifting me bridal style again to carry me off the boat that the full revelation sinks in. Previously, I always had a general idea of my geographical location. All I know based on my concept of time since leaving the main island is that we are still within the lagoon, one of over one hundred islands. It's certainly one of the few islands I've never visited previously.

"The resort is on a private island," Nic whispers as he carefully lowers me to my feet. He refuses to let go of my hand as we follow the concierges into the main lobby to check in. The sudden flurry of activity and the nervousness on the workers' faces reveal their awareness of Nic's position. His smile and tone are reassuring as he confirms the long list of reservations the manager reads. I only catch words here and there, such as "spa" and "class," while I inspect our opulent surroundings. Two hours ago, I was celebrating my wedding on one of the best terraces in the city, yet I'm still taken aback by the luxuries that seem to follow when I'm with him. He slips the room keys in his pocket using the hand that isn't holding mine and graciously thanks the manager before directing his charm back to me.

I keep pace with him as he guides me in the direction of our room. We pass the concierges who had transported our luggage for us, and Nic pauses to tip them. His eyes meet mine in the light of the hallway as he pulls our room key from his pocket. His irises are both darker and more vibrant than usual, but the hunger behind them is unmistakable. The moment our door is closed and locked, his lips are devouring mine in desperation. Until now, I hadn't known how much he had restrained himself, because now there's no hesitation in how quickly he moves. Every kiss and every touch is overwhelming and consuming.

CHAPTER 16

Niccolò

I wake to the peaceful sound of my wife's deep breathing as she sleeps in my arms. The light peeking through the curtains and the clock on the nightstand confirm that it's later in the morning than either of us usually wakes up. Yesterday must have been equally exhausting for both of us. Rather than get up and start my day, I relax against the soft pillows and watch Lina.

"How long are you going to lie there and stare at me like that?" she asks me without opening her eyes.

"For as long as you let me," I respond sappily. That compels her to open her eyes. I expect her to leave the warmth of the bed to get ready for the day, but instead, she snuggles up closer to me.

Thoughtfully, she asks, "What do you think our life would be like if your father were different and my parents were alive and never had to leave?"

"Well, I think we would have grown up together," I tell her as I picture the alternate reality. "Our mothers would have made sure we spent every vacation, holiday, and birthday together. At some point, when we were both old enough to understand, they would tell us that we were to marry each other one day. I would be happy about it because you'd be the prettiest girl I know anyway, and if you weren't happy about it, I'd charm you until you were."

"How exactly would you try to charm me?" she interrupts with an apprehensive expression etched across her face.

I kiss her softly and tenderly, the way I imagine my alternate younger self would kiss her to convince her that the match was certainly to our favor. "Convinced?" I grin.

"You may continue your tale," she replies as she licks her lips. I do my best to ignore my urge to kiss her again and find my train of thought.

"As I was saying before you questioned my charm, I would win you over. We would fall in love with each other as soon as we were mature enough to feel that way. Assuming our mothers were eager to see the marriage become official, the wedding date would likely be anticipated for a few months after your eighteenth birthday. But then they would discover a need to move up the wedding when I'm caught sneaking out of your room."

"Niccolò!" she exclaims as she playfully hits me.

I give her my most innocent look. "Hey, in this scenario, I'm nineteen and desperately in love with my fiancée. Forgive me for not having the self-control to wait a few months. And I most certainly would be caught with how many times I'd been sneaking out."

"Sounds like someone is insatiable," she comments with an eye roll.

I swiftly move my body so that I'm hovering over hers. "Making an heir is one of my main responsibilities at the moment," I say before our lips meet, and I'm lost in her again.

IT'S LATER in the morning when we emerge from our rooms fully dressed, the need for food outweighing the desire to stay in bed all day. The dining room is empty except for a few staff members clearing the last few tables from breakfast. When one of them notices us, he immediately sets up a table for us by the window. Though we've missed the initial breakfast rush, the buffet still holds enough options to fill our plates and stomachs.

The resort and spa on the Sacca Sessola had been Dario's only suggestion for the honeymoon. After a grand wedding where the citizens of Venezia honored and congratulated their prince and princess, a few secluded days with Lina is precisely what I need. The hotel is renowned for luxury, from the private entrance to the fine dining with views of the lagoon. Rather than book the villa for only two people, I opted for the high-end suite with a private pool and terrace. I reserved time slots for several cooking classes, spa treatments, and bike rentals over the next few days. This will be a vacation fit for a future queen.

"I would have made you wait," she says as we sit at the cozy table. My expression must display my confusion. "In that other life where we grew up together, I would make you wait until after the wedding. Being raised as a duchess and future princess, I would have a reputation to uphold, and I could convince our mothers to move the wedding up sooner, without any possible scandal. In this life, I'm glad we waited. If the version of you who lost your mother young is this much of a gentleman, you would have been just as much of one in that other life, too."

"I suppose you're right about that," I say as I reach across the table to squeeze her hand. "Sometimes I wonder how the trip from the castle to Venezia would have been different if you had still been deciding whether or not to kill me."

Her gaze is thoughtful as she ponders the alternate scenario. "I'm not sure if I could have handled that much internal conflict. It took enough willpower not to kiss you. You're the only person I've ever felt that intense an attraction to, especially given how little time we've known each other."

"We're not crazy to get married this quickly," I say to ease whatever worries she may not be voicing. "Dario and Maria dated for about a year, and over that year, they spent maybe five to six hours together each week. If you were to add up all the hours you and I spent together, starting with the night of the ball until we reached Venezia, the total number of hours would be almost the same. Granted, I thought those hours would be the only ones I would get to spend with you, and we were legally betrothed the whole time."

"I can see your logic, though," she says as she looks up from her plate into my eyes. "We essentially took a fast track into marriage. Spending this much time with you doesn't feel strange because we've essentially been around each other almost every day since we met. I don't know if I can bear to be apart from you when you go back to the castle."

I take a deep breath, admonishing myself for assuming this discussion was already resolved. "Lina, the man who currently owns that castle is the same one who tried to kill you. I know that you've sneaked your way in before, but on a routine day, the castle doesn't see many visitors. Can we discuss this after our honeymoon? I want to be fully present with you while we're here instead of worrying about a future that will still be there when our stay is over." Her muscles relax as she temporarily lets this go. There are so many arguments that I will gladly let her win, but anything that jeopardizes her safety is something about which I will never budge. I would rather have her alive and angry with me than anywhere near my father with her identity known.

On our way back to the room, she suggests an afternoon by the infinity pool overlooking the lagoon. Seeing her in a swimsuit is easier this time, or maybe it's merely a different view when she's my wife, because there's no shame or guilt in admiring the woman to whom I've vowed my whole self for all my life.

"Ready?" She turns to me after pulling her curls into a braid. I abandon my observation spot on the other side of the room to pull her into a kiss, careful to keep my hands on her waist.

"I would marry you again today if I could," I say to her with a smile full of happiness.

She takes the initiative to put distance between us. "The pool won't be open later, but anything else you're thinking can wait until then."

I force my body language into the most innocent posture I can muster before grabbing the towels she hands me to carry. While a small part of me might always think about never leaving this hotel room now that she's mine, a larger part of me does want to explore all the amenities the resort and island have to offer. I want to explore everything with her by my side, living the life my mother wanted for me and my father tried to take from me. I want the life with her I could see from the moment I laid eyes on her.

"This is better than I imagined it would be," I say to her as we lounge side by side at the infinity pool.

"An infinity pool that overlooks the lagoon?" Despite her confusion, her tone is playful.

I reach across the narrow gap between our chairs and intertwine our fingers. "A life with you," I say to clarify. "The first time I looked at you, I could see a million memories that hadn't yet happened of the future I wanted with you. It went against all logic to be so certain of a stranger. But this has been so much better than any fantasy." I bring her hand to my mouth and lightly kiss the soft skin.

"For a minute, I wanted to kill you just for making me feel something so intensely," she says in confession. "But then the thought of your eyes losing the light and vibrancy behind them—I never would have released that arrow. You didn't talk me out of it in your chamber because you had already talked me out of it when you helped me off the floor and asked me to dance."

I can still vividly remember her face when I had proposed the innocent question. "You weren't torn over whether or not to dance with me," I say as the realization occurs to me, "you were torn because you knew you couldn't do the one thing you had focused on for most of your life. I feel a bit better about your reaction now that I know the truth."

"Don't let it go to your head. You looked handsome in that suit, but you also seemed like a lost puppy."

We simultaneously shift onto our sides to face each other as I chuckle. "We never talked about how many kids we want," I say to change the topic. "Assuming conceiving isn't the same for us as it was for your parents."

"In a perfect world," she begins before pausing to stop and think, "at least two. I mean, you and your brother both had each other for most of your childhood, and I had Maria. I would want our firstborn to have someone, too."

"Being royalty can be a lonely position," I say as I compare my life before my brother's death and after his passing. When Carlo was around, I had more than just my brother; I had friends and a father who hadn't quite become controlling about our free time. "We'll have as many as you want. I don't have the maximum number, but even two is fine with me. I just wanted to hear your thoughts on the matter since you're the one who has to go through the pregnancies."

She sits up and swings her legs around to the side of her lounger. "Let's start with two and then reevaluate. I'm getting in the pool now. You're welcome to join me or stay here." Of course, I follow closely behind because there isn't anywhere I wouldn't follow her.

THE COOKING CLASS at the Sapori Cooking Academy is reminiscent of the times we've cooked dinner together on our stops back to Venezia from the castle. We already have an efficient pattern and method for splitting the tasks. The others in the class don't display the same level of teamwork, but the instructor insists it's not a competition. Lina's competitive nature is reason enough for me to ignore the teacher and help my wife "win" in whatever way I can. There isn't much thrill for her in the end, though, so an hour after dinner, we're side by side on exercise bikes in the fitness center.

Realistically, the day of our wedding and the day that followed were both rest days for her. I even start to feel restless now, having had too long a break after the training routine I followed both with Lina and Franco, and then with Dario. Less than twelve hours from now, we'll be back here to exercise before the couples massage I reserved at the spa. I prepaid for almost every treatment they offer, knowing that she won't refuse something already purchased. The estate in Siena is likely nice given its duchy ownership, but it won't have the same luxuries as the castle. This is my best chance to spoil her for the foreseeable future.

"Is the couples massage one in which we both receive a massage at the same time or the type where it's essentially a class where we're taught how to give each other a massage?" Lina asks me at breakfast. The possibility of the latter option is one I hadn't considered, and certainly not one I would want supervised.

"The former, and it's in a couple's suite," I say, resisting the temptation to rub away the wrinkle she gets between her eyebrows when she's trying to solve a puzzle in her head. "I opted for the intense muscle release treatment since it seemed more fitting for us."

She visibly relaxes against her chair with both her hands cradling her cappuccino. I wish I could forever savor the blissful expression on her face, and we haven't even gotten our massages yet. This escape from the outside world of corrupt government and the Resistance is fleeting and temporary. Eventually, we'll return to a country in which the crown prince and his bride are at odds with the reigning monarch. Once we return to the main island, we have one more day for final preparations and goodbyes before the long drive back to the villa outside Napoli for one night. The short stays to come are the price to pay for this honeymoon.

While we lay side by side on the massage tables, I imagine a scenario in which I can bring her back here every year for our anniversary. It had seemed impossible, but so had the idea of being with her for the rest of my life at many points on this journey.

"How was the island?" Dario asks us as he greets us at the dock. I spent the entire boat ride mesmerized by my wife's glow under the morning sunlight.

"I hope that's where you're planning to take Maria," Lina says in answer. "They have their own olive oil that they grow on the island and use in the kitchens and spa. If the Siena estate doesn't already have olive trees, we should cultivate some there."

Before Dario can climb aboard to carry her suitcase, she's already loading it onto the dock. He turns to me and shrugs helplessly, as if he's surprised she would still be this independent after her years of training for a solo mission. She walks ahead of us toward the Bauer Palazzo, our lodging for our last night in the city. Despite the slight distance, neither of us trusts the space to be enough to ensure a private conversation. Maria waits for us at one of the hotel's restaurants, wrapping Lina in a hug when she sees her sister. Dario and I offer to take the bags up to the room while they catch up, but they're both engrossed enough in their excitement that neither acknowledges us.

"Are you disappointed to no longer be on the island?" Dario questions when we're alone in the elevator.

"No," I say before deciding to elaborate. "It's easy when you're in a bubble like on the island, but bubbles always pop eventually. The time together was a necessity. In hindsight, I'm baffled that people can endure engagements that last a year or longer. Two weeks felt like torture at times when all I wanted to be was married to her."

Dario smiles wryly and says, "Not all of us are in quite the same circumstances as you are in, either. I'm just glad there was availability for the terrace Maria wanted three months from now. Three months should be enough time for you two to settle in at the Siena base before traveling back here for another wedding."

"Hopefully, there's a larger gap of time before Franco's wedding," I say thoughtfully. "I'm a bit weary of living out of my suitcase, and this is only a fraction of what I'll have to pack when I stop by the castle."

"I don't envy you there," he says as he leads me out of the hotel room and back to our significant others. Though she doesn't shift her gaze away from Maria when we rejoin them, Lina's face lights up when I hold her hand.

The remainder of our final full day in Venezia consists of an afternoon at the Resistance base, dinner with Lina's parents, and strolls through the maze of streets and canals. We stop at Dario's cousin's gelato shop. Everyone here is aware of the wedding by now, and he gives us the gelato as a late wedding gift. Once we're out of the shop with our stracciatella cones, I whisper, "Beautiful Lina" in her ear. She blushes and kisses me on the cheek. When we pass by a blown glass boutique, I insist on browsing at the colored works of art before buying Lina a pair of earrings the same blue as the lagoon's water.

Once we're alone again for the night, the happy expression on her face slips. She's not leaving on a short-term mission to assassinate a prince this time; she's moving to start a life that will end with a crown. The Sozzini estate might be Resistance-occupied and highly secure, but it's still the house of a noble family with marriage ties to the royal line. Meeting me has changed her life in an entirely irreversible way. Lina can never go back to who she was before she met me.

"I love you," she says as if I could ever forget. "It's just a little strange to be leaving here again in such a condensed period. It almost feels as if I just left the first time, and it's a strange sense of déjà vu."

"You make me so unreasonably happy," I say in response, and it's enough to bring back some of the brightness to her mood.

THE FASTEST ROUTE from the Resistance's fleet station on Tronchetto to the villa north of Napoli is approximately seven hours of driving. Initially, we had debated the pros and cons of Maria sitting in the back seat with Lina. With the sunrise painting the backdrop behind the Piasa San Marco, it provided scintillating conversation over breakfast. Ultimately, the fastest route involves skirting around larger cities, including Bologna, Firenze, and the capital city of Roma. The other two possible routes add forty to fifty extra minutes to what would already be a long drive. In the end, it was agreed that driving that close to the castle with my face viewable in the front seat was too big a risk. Those risks are also why we stop for lunch at a restaurant on the outskirts of Chiusi, far enough away from the train station to avoid as many unknown factors as possible. We stretch our legs and relish the fresh Tuscan air for an hour before piling back into the sleek black Resistance-owned SUV.

The conversation among the four of us flows easily as if I'm just as much one of them now. I'm not a fourth wheel among three friends who have years of bonding to tie them together; I belong in a way I didn't know I longed for until I had it. Lina's hand never leaves mine once I intertwine our fingers. The physical touch makes me grateful I'm not in the front passenger seat. Tomorrow, Lina is traveling with Dario and Maria to Siena, while I go to the castle alone. My heart already hurts at the thought of being away from her temporarily.

From the end of the driveway, the villa appears the same as we left it, my car parked in the exact spot I noted before leaving with Lina and Franco weeks ago. Lina and Maria stay in the SUV while Dario and I scan the perimeter around the grounds, followed by the security sweep inside. Though I'm confident Lina could hold her own if there were somehow an ambush waiting for us, I'm grateful she's with Maria in the car. As we had hoped, the house remains untouched from when we departed. Dario offers to drive into the city to pick up a few fresh fruits and vegetables for us while Lina and I give Maria the grand tour in his absence.

"I almost wish we were staying here longer," she says with a sigh and a longing gaze at the pool.

As we circle through the house, Lina adds her comments. At the entrance to the study, she points and tells Maria, "That corner is where I almost kissed Nic the first time."

"There's something to be said about two people who almost kissed as frequently as you two seemed to," Maria says with a shake of her head. "It's certainly for the best that you're married now."

Dario yells to alert us of his return, and Maria excuses herself to help him in the kitchen with the produce. When Lina's gaze shifts to me, I silently motion to the corner before leading her there to follow through on what I couldn't that night.

LINA and I volunteer to prepare dinner, giving Dario and Maria time to enjoy the pool during their only night here. While Lina and I work around each other in the kitchen, I imagine what it would have been like to have our mothers here with us. It would be impossible to get through dinner without some mention of how excited they are for grandchildren.

"Are you still dead set against my coming to the castle with you?" Lina asks, bringing me back into this reality. I'm surprised it took her this long to bring it up again.

"Is it so absurd that I would put your safety above anything else?" I say in answer to her question.

"I'm capable of staying safe," she insists. "I'm the one who snuck into your bed chamber on a night when security at the castle was at its highest. It just feels like you're treating me like I'm some delicate princess or duchess or whatever rather than your almost-assassin and one of the highest-ranked Resistance agents."

Frustration marks her expression, a reflection of my own emotions. I'm not frustrated with her; I'm frustrated that she can't see my perspective on this. I try to find the words to explain my reasoning to her. "Lina, I'm trying to treat you like you're my wife and partner. It's not your abilities or skills that I'm worried about. I'm worried about the slight chance that your coming with me could result in my losing you, and I don't know if I could bear it if something happened to you. You're my family, my home, my everything. It's entirely selfish of me, but I can't lose you."

His confession is what finally breaks down the walls of my foolish stubbornness. I don't even know why I was being obstinate about this. Deep down, I know he has good intentions behind his decision, but I pushed anyway when I didn't like the answer. I knew that if I didn't fight him on this the first time, I wouldn't have as much of a say when he takes trips to the castle in the future.

"If you think that going alone is the best thing to ensure we both survive, then I trust you," I say to him, wrapping my arms around him in an embrace. "As much as I hate the idea of being away from you for days or even weeks, I would hate it more if I came and the worst did happen. I had backup with me when I went to the ball, and I hadn't even thought about the fact that I wouldn't have that if I came with you. Everyone is expecting me to be at the Siena base tomorrow."

"One day, we'll be able to walk into that castle together as the rulers of this kingdom," he says into my hair.

"Are you two finally done fighting?" Dario asks as he pulls the entrée out of the oven. Neither of us had noticed Dario's presence, but Nic doesn't even jump at the silent entrance like he once did.

I rest my head on Nic's chest and relish the feeling of home his nearness brings. I say, "I wouldn't call it a fight. It was merely a disagreement over whether we must go in different directions tomorrow. I'm dreading being away from him." What I don't admit is my nervousness about returning to a family estate I can't remember. Though I won't have my husband by my side, Dario and Maria will be enough to keep the anxiety at bay.

"Be safe," I whisper as I cling to his torso. "I don't know what I would do if I lost you now."

"Hey, I'll be okay," he promises as he kisses my hair. "You and I keep beating the odds. It's all thanks to that statue of Giulietta."

I lightly punch his arm. "You do realize that Romeo and Giulietta got married in secret before they both died tragically, right? We're not out of the woods yet by those standards. I can promise you that I will never let you believe that I'm dead. Although ironically, my parents and an entire alliance against the throne led your father to believe I wasn't alive."

"Perhaps we should stop comparing ourselves to a couple who didn't get to spend the rest of their lives together," he suggests before his lips meet mine, a soft and tender "until later."

"I love you," I say, the words as natural as breathing.

"I love you, and I'll see you soon."

Reluctantly, I release my hold on him and watch as he climbs into his Maserati, the engine purring despite its inactivity for the last few weeks. I stand outside as my heart drives away, heading back to the castle to tie up loose ends. Dario and Maria sit in the front seats of the Resistance SUV, waiting for me. Once I'm in the backseat with my seatbelt fastened, Dario follows the same route. Despite the castle being on the way to our destination, Dario and Nic agreed that Nic should have a few minutes of a head start to avoid any suspicion of our vehicles traveling together.

"I'm excited about seeing the Siena base," Maria says to take my mind off the visceral separation from my husband. "This is like being an honorary member of the Resistance."

"Just because you're not an agent doesn't mean you're not part of the Resistance," Dario says. "And you're an agent by proxy because you're marrying me."

We spend the four-hour drive making both real and absurd assumptions about the estate and any renovations that have been made since Director Verde reclaimed the Sozzini inheritance. By name, neither she nor I is a Sozzini given my recent change of name. What I hadn't been expecting was for the estate to be enclosed within stone walls with a gate, as if it were a medieval fortress. In hindsight, Zeta's description of the base in Tuscany should have tipped me off to this possibility. The guard at the gate recognizes Dario from a special training a few years ago.

He asks, "Would you like us to address you as Her Royal Highness?" It takes me a moment to realize the question was for me.

"Please, just call me Lina," I practically beg. He seems relieved at the permission to address me casually and waves us through to the driveway leading to the main house. When we're on the other side of the outer walls, the extent of the estate finally comes into view. The original house is the largest building on the property, though the base facility is a similar size. On the other side of the base lie smaller houses, likely belonging to the agents who reside here. Small fields of vines and olive trees line either side of the drive, which is hedged in by the iconic cypress trees of Tuscany. My skin tingles with the buzz of anticipation as it had the day of the ball at the castle.

Dario pulls the SUV to the front of the main house and shifts the gear into park, but none of us rush to venture inside. We bask in the moment of calm, knowing that the remainder of the day holds anything but. Finally, I'm the first to open the door and slip into the summer air. My actions must have burst the bubble because seconds later, agents surrounded us with introductions and helped carry the majority of my belongings into the house. A few minutes later, it's clear that one of them is directing the action.

"My name is Bria, and I'll be your assistant, Your Highness," she says to me once the others are clear on their assignments. Looking at her face, I wouldn't guess her to be more than twenty, but she carries herself in a way that's both humble and confident. I wonder if Zeta had chosen her specifically to be my aid.

"Please call me Lina," I say and plaster a friendly smile across my face. "Be sure to tell the others that as well. My husband will have to confirm this when he arrives, but I suspect he would also prefer less formality."

"Very well, Lina," Bria says as she turns her attention to my companions. "And you must be Dario and Maria. Come, let me give you the official tour of the estate." We follow her lead into the house where my parents and grandparents once resided. Strangers are more familiar with my inheritance than I am, but from now on, that changes.

The exterior of the house is nothing compared to the opulence inside. In every bedroom suite, chandeliers hang from the ceilings, detailed in designs of crown molding. Despite the house's age, the kitchen and bathrooms were recently remodeled, likely within the last few years. Even with the decadence and space I'm not accustomed to, it still feels comfortable, the way I'd felt returning to Venezia after my travels across the country. It's the strange conflict of being both new yet familiar. To my delight, the back of the house has a pool, patio, jacuzzi, and multi-level gardens. Bria continues the tour to the newer additions on the estate, the Resistance training center. The headquarters in Venezia has mazes of hallways that mirror the streets and canals of the city; this base is reminiscent of a village with offices and private rooms surrounding the larger core of exercise machines and sparring arenas. One of those offices has my name etched in the plate fastened to the door.

"Will your husband require his own office?" Bria asks me as she opens the door and gestures into the spacious room.

It feels strange to make this decision without him here, but I selfishly answer, "No, I think we'll be more productive sharing this one. Thank you, though, Bria." On our way out of the training center, she instructs another agent to arrange for another desk and chair to be brought into the director's office.

"Are you sure you want to share an office with Nic?" Dario asks me quietly. Both he and Maria have remained quiet during the estate tour. Periodically, I turned around to ensure they were still following me and Bria.

"I think it would be ideal for now, at least while we're finding our bearings," I say in equally low volume. "He's still new to the Resistance, while I'm new to leading. He may not be the king, but he's certainly been trained in how to manage a country. I have no idea how to run an entire estate." Being a long-lost duchess has its drawbacks.

Bria ends the tour by showing us to our suites. Dario and Maria both have their own guest suites, but mine is the master suite. Once I'm alone in the bedroom that once belonged to my parents, I open doors, discovering the connected nursery. It's as if time stood still with everything nearly untouched and unmoved. Whoever cleaned did so carefully. I half expect to see an infant in the cradle, but that baby has outgrown it now. Tears flow of their own volition as I mourn what I've lost and celebrate what I've gained. This house is now mine, as it always should have been. I'm married to Prince Niccolò as our mothers had intended. Whatever caused King Vincenzo to target my family had to be significant. He wouldn't have harmed his beloved wife's closest friend over something trivial. Part of me will always be restless until I uncover the whole truth.

"Lina, I just got a call from the guard at the front gate," Dario says, clearly in a rush. "He's here, and I'm going to confirm his identity."

Finally, everything I had been focused on ten seconds ago is no longer important. Niccolò is here. When I stand, Maria tugs on my arm as a gesture to ask me to stay here. After I couldn't sleep well alone in my large bed the first night here, Maria has been sharing the master suite with me. In many ways, having her close felt like it had during our childhood. She helped me unpack my belongings and organize what little was left behind from my parents. While I appreciate the time I've gotten with her here in Siena, it wasn't enough to distract me from his absence. Not knowing how long—not being able to count down the days—was the hardest part. Sometimes, I would pray for his safety, unsure if my pleas could be heard by God, whom I didn't know as well as I should. Nic is here.

Unable to sit still, I walk to the front door of the main house as Maria and Bria follow close behind. I pace and wait. Down the driveway, I see the approaching Resistance SUV followed by the familiar dark blue Maserati. He's really here. Once the vehicles are both parked, the unmistakable figure of my husband emerges from the car, his eyes fixed on me. Somehow, I resist the urge to run to him as he forgoes whatever luggage may be in his car and beelines for me.

"Hi," he says with his charming prince smile.

"Hi," I say breathlessly before my hands fly around his neck to pull him into a kiss. For a few moments, I forget we're not alone and allow myself to focus on him. Through the haze of our reunion, I catch snippets of Bria instructing someone to carry the prince's bags to the master suite.

"This estate is impressive," he says once we've returned from our own world to our surroundings.

I move my hands from his neck so I can hold his hand. "Let me give you the official tour."

Weeks of disrupted routine catch up to us, resulting in late mornings more often than not. Lina trains six days a week, and I follow her lead, finding myself growing stronger and faster. The other agents at the base treat us as equals, as if we're co-directors. While I appreciate the sentiment, I know I didn't earn their respect the way Lina has with her years of service. The two parts of our lives, the agents versus the prince and princess, almost contradict each other. Sometimes, I imagine we're merely the duke and duchess of the estate, though I would always hold the title of a prince, even if I hadn't become the crown prince.

At the training center, we share an office. It's still unclear to me whether it was Zeta's choice or Lina's, but it proves to be the most productive solution the majority of the time. We work well together, occasionally a little too well, but she's the master of creating and respecting boundaries. I'm so used to Lina's high-intensity lifestyle that it alarms me when she decides to rest two days in a row.

"Too much change too quickly?" I ask her without masking my concern.

"Maybe," she says uncertainly. "I just know I'm not feeling one hundred percent. I might go for a swim later to make up for it." Despite her best intentions, it doesn't reassure me. When Bria asks if I need her to pick up anything from town for my next journey back to the castle, the day after tomorrow, I add one thing to the list.

Though I'm rarely in the training center without Lina, it's easy to get into a rhythm as I start my usual circuit, the routine allowing me to silence my mind for a few hours. The consistency of a schedule like this is easy; I understand Lina, Dario, and Franco in a way I hadn't before. The male agents who had once been standoffish around me have gradually warmed to me, likely realizing that I'm not quite the expert that Lina and Dario both are. With some skills, I know the technique but lack the effortless execution that comes with training six days a week for years. It's never too late to catch up to their level.

On my way back to the main house, I walk around the back to the pool, hoping to find my wife. The empty yet inviting water glistens with the sun's reflection. I walk into the kitchen and catch Bria putting away the groceries she brought from town.

"Bria, did you find what I asked for?" I ask as I suddenly remember my unusual request.

"I left it in the master suite," she says nonchalantly. "I think Lina was up there, if you're looking for her."

Without another word, I dash to our shared bedroom. I hadn't yet explained my suspicions to Lina, and this is quite possibly the worst way for me to do so. When I reach the door, I knock before entering to alert her to my presence. She's sitting on the bed, holding the box. I can't read her expression to gauge her thoughts or mood, but I close the door for the inevitable private conversation.

"You asked Bria to pick this up from town?" I can't decipher whether the question she directs at me is rhetorical. I choose silence rather than giving the obvious answer. Lina continues, "I can't believe I didn't even think of this possibility."

"You've been tired and your appetite has been all over the place lately," I say to give her my reasoning. "It could be stress, but I know you would want to know otherwise. We may need to see a doctor. You should probably go to one sooner than I'll be back from my next stint at the castle."

She sighs as she flips the box of pregnancy tests over in her hands. "I haven't had a period since right before the wedding. At first, I thought it might be stress and all the changes. It seemed silly to assume this when it took my mother so long to conceive. I suppose I should take the test."

"I'm right here no matter what the result is."

Lina's small smile doesn't hide her nerves as she goes into our bathroom. I lie across our bed and close my eyes as I hear her rummage around the adjoining room. Minutes later, she emerges with a timer in one hand. After setting it down on the nightstand, she lies down next to me and curls up against me like she does in her sleep.

My hand draws lazy circles across the smooth skin of her forearm as I say, "No matter what the result is, I'm content."

"I was just starting to feel like I was adjusting to life here on the estate," she says, her breath deep and steady. "I've barely started going through all the books in the library about my family's history. I'm still baffled that the Resistance managed to keep that much hidden from your father. There's so much I don't know about where I came from, and I'm hoping there's something there that can help piece together your father's unexplained animosity toward the Sozzinis. At the same time, though, I've been worried about the fertility problems my mother had. I don't know what I want the result to be."

I kiss her forehead in response, fully understanding her apprehension. As we wait for the timer to go off, we're interrupted by a knock at the door.

"I'm sorry to bother you, but there's someone at the estate entrance insisting he needs to see you, Prince Niccolò," Bria says apologetically.

I look to Lina, about to request that she stay here while I check to see who could be asking for an audience with me, but I can see by her expression that she won't be leaving my side. My mind races with the possibilities as Bria leads us toward our visitor. If it were my father, the agents would recognize him and be on higher alert than they seem to be. Whoever this is has to be a stranger to the Resistance agents keeping watch over the estate. That, or he's someone they're very familiar with.

When I see him, I think my eyes must be playing tricks on me. Flanked by Resistance agents, I glimpse a man who looks as though he were manifested from my memories. Despite the shock, I put one foot in front of the other to close the distance.

"It's been a while, brother," Carlo says with a smirk.

TO BE CONTINUED…

Acknowledgments

Let me start by saying that I did not plan for this to be the fifth book I would publish. I had another book in mind that I thought would be the fifth book because I wanted to have a better idea of the plot for the sequel to this before releasing it into the world. However, life intervened, and I had to step back from that other story. Naturally, editing this was the obvious course of action if I wanted to continue releasing books. I did not anticipate it would take me as long as it did to have this in your hands.

I drafted this story during National Novel Writing Month in 2021. If I remember correctly, I didn't get the idea for this story until the last week of October. I spent weeks brainstorming, and this popped into my head at the last minute. Of all the NaNoWriMo stories I want to publish, this was the least well-outlined and thought-through. Realistically, I only had a plot twist that won't even occur until the sequel. The others happened of their own accord.

This is my first time releasing a book that isn't a standalone, and I needed my beta readers to help spot any plot holes. Some questions remain unanswered because diving into that part of the story would have made this too long a story for one novel. Thank you to Erica and Danny Raye for your constructive criticism. Getting this up to par required more rewriting than anticipated, but I needed to give the readers my best stab at telling the first part of this tale. Thank you to my writer's accountability group for forcing me to set realistic goals for continuing my writing, editing, and publishing.

Thank you to my readers for your patience. You likely caught all the times I said "didn't anticipate." God has a way of redirecting, and I needed to trust His timing with this one. I expected the number of books I release in a year would decrease to one; however, I didn't know when that would occur. Writing isn't my main job at this point in my life, nor is it my only hobby. If all I did was write in my free time, I wouldn't be living a life that inspires more books. I want my books to inspire you to live and hope in a way that motivates you to do the things that make you come alive.

And about that cliffhanger...sorry, not sorry.

Abridged Autobiography

As a second-generation American, I share a love for both my country and for all the places abroad that I haven't seen yet or that I want to see again. It doesn't help that I have enough nationalities mixed into my genetics that I have yet to see all the places my ancestors are from.

I love to read and write almost as much as I love all things Italian–the food, the language, the country, the leather, the coffee, the food, and the list goes on. The slight obsession with Italy is evident in my stories. My preferred schedule is that of a night owl, though I'm adaptable when necessary as long as I have caffeine. When I'm not lost in another world or country, Kansas City is home and the Chiefs are my NFL team.

Jesus is an essential part of my life and identity and a big reason why I keep on writing happy endings. Sometimes I write as a way to balance the power between my imagination and the logical part of my brain, the side that tries to remain tethered to reality.

lbethcampbell.com

For updates on future releases, sign up for my monthly email
newsletter through my website and follow me on Instagram

@L.BethCampbell

Also by L. Beth Campbell

The Trophy Wife's User Guide

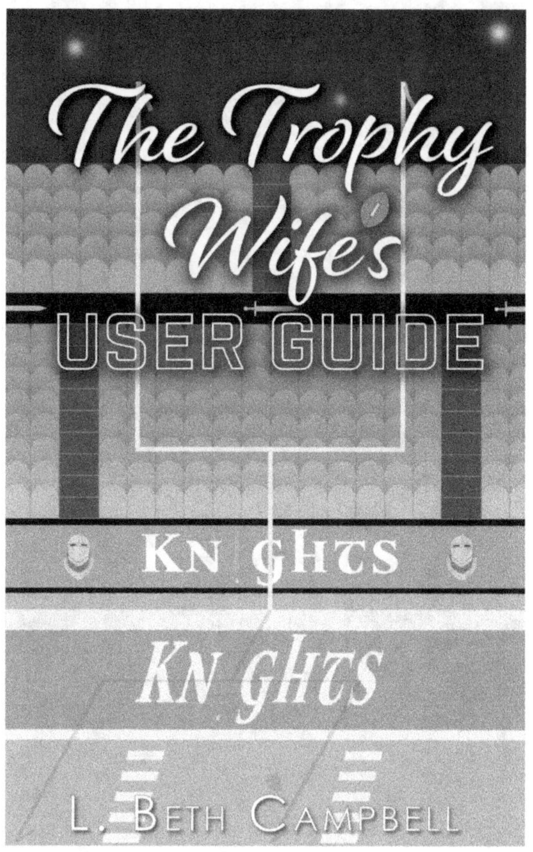

At Second
Sight
L. BETH CAMPBELL

Kissing
the
Blarney
Stone
L. BETH CAMPBELL

The Arranged
Crown
L. BETH CAMPBELL

www.ingramcontent.com/pod-product-compliance
Lightning Source LLC
Chambersburg PA
CBHW070503300726

48975CB00007B/2303